T0129487

The Last
President

The Last
President

ISIS ATTACKS

REG IVORY

iUniverse®

THE LAST PRESIDENT
ISIS ATTACKS

iUniverse books may be ordered through booksellers or by contacting:

iUniverse
1663 Liberty Drive
Bloomington, IN 47403
www.iuniverse.com
1-800-Authors (1-800-288-4677)

ISBN: 978-1-5320-0395-0 (sc)
ISBN: 978-1-5320-0396-7 (hc)
ISBN: 978-1-5320-0397-4 (e)

Library of Congress Control Number: 2016914718

Print information available on the last page.

iUniverse rev. date: 09/07/2016

I'll tell you what war is about, you've got to kill people, and when you've killed enough they stop fighting.

—US Air Force General Curtis LeMay,
Strategic Air Command

And the Congress may by law provide for the case wherein neither a President elect nor a Vice President elect shall have qualified, declaring who shall then act as President, or the manner in which one who is to act shall be selected, and such person shall act accordingly until a President or Vice President shall have qualified.

—The Twentieth Amendment to the
United States Constitution, Section 3

Section 1: When the Congress shall have declared who shall act as President under Article XX, Section 3, the Congress shall additionally provide for the interim general election of a President as soon as practical but, in no case, no later than two years after the acting President shall have assumed office.

Section 2. The Congress, under Article V, shall propose this Amendment to the Constitution by a joint resolution of two-thirds vote of both Houses. A letter of notification of this proposed Amendment shall then be sent immediately, preferably by electronic means, to each of the several states for ratification by their State Legislatures.

Section 3. Provided however that the several states are not required to wait for official notice of the passing of the joint resolution before taking action. Ratification of this proposed Amendment, under Article V, shall be by Legislatures of three fourths of the several States. Upon approval, states shall, without delay, initiate procedures to prepare for a general election to elect a President who shall serve until the next regularly scheduled general election.

Section 4. This proposed amendment shall take effect immediately upon approval by the states.

—Proposed Twenty-Eighth Amendment to the
United States Constitution

1

ABDUL ANWAR ALI, FORMER PRESIDENT for life of Syria, looked around his filthy, squalid hut on the Syrian-Lebanese border and cursed his life and his enemies for the millionth time. It was fortunate he had no mirror to see his appearance. Tattered rags covered his body, once clothed in the finest silks. His beard was untrimmed and hung well below his stomach. It had been months since he had bathed, and his own scent often sickened him—he, Ali, who had once been bathed two or three times a day by the most enticing women. How could he have come to this end—living and eating like a pig, afraid to be seen, knowing the Israelis, the Americans, and their allies continued to hunt for him?

How long had it been now since the war? A year? Two? He had completely lost track of time. Occasionally, he could hear the sounds of battle in the distance. But who was fighting whom? The ignorant peasant family he lived with knew nothing of politics or the military. And so he lived in ignorance. How could it have gone so badly, so quickly? Now he, the *Soul of the Sword*, once the most feared man in the Middle East, had been reduced to less than nothing. He looked down at the stinking, fat peasant girl who had spent the night, a "gift" from the family who protected him—Ali, who had had his choice of some of the most exquisite women in the world. He cursed again and kicked the girl until she farted loudly, awoke, and left the hut.

He heard sounds of a truck outside and prepared himself, once more, for the possibility of capture. They would never take him alive.

He was armed and would rather die than be displayed in public, judged, and executed. He uncovered his 9 mm Makarov pistol, a gift from the Russian president during a visit to Ali at his palace in Damascus before the war. And where had that impertinent little dog been when Ali had requested help? Where had they all been—his allies? Ali spat and made certain the pistol was loaded and ready.

Two men entered the hut, dressed in Arabic garb, their faces covered. They both had automatic weapons, American made. So it would be the American infidels who finally came for him. Ali raised his weapon. He would kill at least one of them before taking his own life.

"As-salaam alaikum," the taller of the two men said. "Peace be upon you." Both men laid down their weapons.

What trick is this? Ali thought. These men could be anyone. He had so many enemies. And there was a price of five million on his head. "Who are you?" he asked, trying to show no fear, his pistol still raised.

The tall man removed his facial covering. His beard was dark black and closely trimmed. Even in the dim light, Ali could see his gleaming eyes. In other times, he would have thought these eyes to be those of a prophet—if there were prophets. Clearly, this man was different. His Arabic garments were traditional but of a higher class than those of an ordinary commoner. His manner of speaking was also cultured.

"I am Abu Bakr, the caliph of the Islamic State. And I am here to free you and restore your honor and power, in the sacred name of Allah, praise be upon him."

Ali knew this could be nothing more than trickery. "I have never heard of you, and the term *caliph* has not been used in my country in a thousand years. And what is the Islamic State?"

The tall man smiled down at Ali. "Many things have been altered since the last war, my brother, and I know it has been difficult for you to keep track of the changes. Guided by the prophet Muhammad, bless his holy name, my followers and I have formed a new army in what was Syria and Iraq. Now we cover the Middle East and many other parts of the world. We are in a battle to the death with the Americans and the West, and we are winning. I have come to restore your honor and to ask that you join us. Everything else will be explained later."

Ali was still not convinced. "How can I be certain you are a brother and not an infidel?"

The man reached down to a sack he had thrown on the ground, opened it, pulled out a human head, and held it up to the light. "Do you recognize this face?"

Ali was not shocked. He had beheaded many men and women himself. He stood and came closer. The horrid, blood-smeared face was vaguely familiar. "I cannot be certain."

The man threw the head down on the dirt floor. "This was the American counsel in Syria, who you entertained many times. His name was Robert Blake."

For the first time, Ali smiled. Of course, it was Blake, a man he had never liked. Ali had even offered the man one of his most beautiful women during Blake's visit to the palace, and the man had refused—a grievous offense.

"This pig looks better without a body, lying on the floor of this disgusting hut."

"I agree. A place you will no longer be forced to tolerate if you agree to join us."

The truth was that Ali had few options. He no longer had power, followers, an army, or weapons. Whoever this man was who called himself a caliph, Ali could do no worse. "If you are doing as well as you say, why are you coming to me? What can I possibly add to your organization?"

"You are the former president for life of Syria, a man who was feared and followed by thousands of our brothers. You would bring us strength and honor. If I should fall in battle, you would lead our caliphate and continue the fight. I can promise you the latest arms, safety, and beautiful women for your pleasure. You will also stand beside me as an equal in the coming Islamic State and have an assured place in heaven, my brother. There is also this." The man pulled aside his cloak and drew a golden sword from his belt. "For you," he said, holding it out to Ali, "the Soul of the Sword."

Ali was speechless. This was his personal sword, a symbol of his former office. He was certain this was a sign directly from Allah.

Accepting his sword, he bowed and offered his pistol to the tall man. "In the name of Allah, I will join you in your fight."

The two men embraced.

Bakr, Ali, and the two guards waited in the hut until dark. They had much to discuss, and Bakr brought Ali up to date on what had been happening in the world since the last war, when Ali had barely escaped from the Western allies. When night had fallen and the desert was a sea of darkness, the men walked out to a camouflaged SUV hidden in a shed, removed the cover, and began their journey.

"We have only two hundred miles to travel, Ali," Bakr said. "But we must be careful. The Americans have aircraft that patrol at night, and they search for single vehicles like this to destroy. We chose this moonless night to return to our stronghold, and we will stop at several locations to sleep and eat and refresh ourselves."

Ali nodded. "I see that your men drive without lights, Caliph. Are they choosing directions by the stars?"

"To some degree, Ali. But they know this desert like the hairs on their heads. They will find our way and keep us secure. Try to get some sleep now, my friend. We will arrive at our next safe place in two hours."

2

ACTING PRESIDENT ROSE AKRON STOOD looking out from the Oval Office onto the south lawn of the White House. She recalled seeing a photo of President Kennedy in a similar pensive mood. "I wonder what you were thinking then, Jack," she said aloud. "Probably not what I'm thinking now."

The presidency inevitably aged those who held the office. But the changes in Akron since she had been appointed by Congress eighteen months ago were shocking to those who had known her before. Only forty-three, her hair had turned completely gray, and her facial lines seemed deeper every day. She wore no makeup, and people often asked if she had been ill. Never one to dress extravagantly, Akron now wore drab, unsophisticated clothing that did nothing to improve her image.

The Oval Office became a reflection of the woman. She had made no changes since President Pete Danzig had completed his term and departed Washington. She'd kept the furnishings, carpeting, and a few of the standard photographs of the Capitol and prominent Washington monuments. Her only contribution was a framed copy of section three of the Twentieth Amendment, which authorized Congress to select an acting president when no one had qualified for the office. Congress had chosen her, an inexperienced, first-term congresswoman from Minnesota, and now she found herself in the Oval Office.

Akron shook her head, sat down at her desk, and pushed a switch that would bring her chief of staff, Sherman Boyle, into the room. After her fifteen combative months in office, Boyle was one of the few people she could trust.

"Good morning, Madam President," Boyle said, entering from one of three seamless doorways to the Oval Office. His bright smile and green tie, embossed with a prominent shamrock, had become his trademarks.

"Sherm, I've told you from the beginning, you can call me Rose."

Boyle grinned at his boss and sat down across from her. "It lessens the prestige of the office, Madam President, an office to which you were legally appointed by the Congress."

Akron sighed and made a poor attempt to smooth her hair. "Let's get to something that's really important. What's the latest in the Middle East?

"Some things never change, Madam President. ISIS still has us stymied. We hit them in one place, and they attack in three others. Their troops are quick, well trained, and well equipped." He paused for a moment. "You've seen the action reports from our field commanders. Something big is brewing over there. We're using every source we have to find out more."

The acting president shook her head and moved some meaningless files around on her desk. "I got the same feeling from those reports and from the Joint Chiefs. Yesterday, ISIS threatened another attack on Washington, DC. Something has to give. I'll speak to General Courier about this later today. Now, what's this I hear about a call for an interim election for president?"

"Unlikely. Boss, there would have to be a constitutional amendment calling for a special election, and that must be passed by the legislatures of thirty-eight states."

The president nodded. "I've heard that our old friend, former Speaker Lucy Jennings, has drafted just such an amendment."

Boyle agreed. "I've heard the same thing. But if it exists, no one has seen it yet. Besides, Lucy Jennings has no power and very little support."

"But she does have some support, Sherm, and plenty of personal money. She keeps saying she was the first person nominated by the former House to be acting president before I got"—she smiled—"before I got so lucky."

Akron looked out of her window again. "By the way, Sherm, what would it take to pass an amendment like that?"

Boyle opened a folder in his lap. "The most likely scenario is through a proposal by the Congress with a two-thirds vote in both Houses. Then they'd send it to the states for ratification. Right now, I don't see that removing you from office is enough of a hot issue."

"And when was the last time there was an issue that was hot enough?"

Boyle laughed. "Repealing prohibition."

Akron finally smiled. "What about the president? Don't I have a role in this?"

"Nope. None at all. The proposed amendment becomes part of the Constitution as soon as it is ratified by three-fourths of the states—that's thirty-eight. Since most of the state legislatures now vote by secured computers, it could take only weeks. Or even days."

"That's comforting." Akron looked closely at her chief of staff. "I see you've been keeping up to date on the process, Sherm."

"Just doing my job, Madam President. And even if all of this came to pass, how long might it take to determine how to select candidates to run for the office? Who decides? As you know, normally that process could take a year or two. Your appointment would be up by then."

"I have a gut feeling we'll hear more about this. I've learned that Washington loves intrigue, Sherm. And nothing is more intriguing than presidential politics. Find out what Lucy Jennings has been up to. See if you can get hold of a copy of this proposed amendment of hers."

"I'm on it. And look on the bright side, boss. There haven't been any calls for your impeachment."

Rose frowned. "I heard the Senate majority leader say that's only because I haven't done a damn thing since being appointed acting president, so there's nothing to be impeached for."

"Sticks and stones, Madam President. Sticks and stones."

The president stood, and Boyle quickly did the same. "Thank you, Madam President," he said as he left the room.

Akron sighed and again stared out the window of the Oval Office. The tense, anxious mood throughout this new Congress was just right for strong, even radical change because of a growing war in the Middle

East and a do-nothing government. Since she had been sworn in, she'd had little support in either the House or the Senate and received constant criticism from politicians in both parties, as well as from a good deal of the American people. The word on Akron was that she was simply not tough enough.

Akron's thoughts turned again to an option she had previously rejected several times. Resignation. After all, she was under verbal attack from her own country, as well as real attacks by ISIS around the world. She had little experience and no solid constituency support. Her personal life had deteriorated too.

Turning to the folders on her desk, she forced the idea out of her mind once again—at least for the time being.

3

FORMER HOUSE SPEAKER LUCY JENNINGS pushed the elevator button of the exclusive Reagan Apartment complex, glancing briefly at her reflected image in the brass elevator doors. Jennings was often referred to as *stunning* in gossipy media accounts, and speculation abounded concerning who she was bedding and whether or not her body was refurbished from time to time. Her five-foot-seven frame was lean but muscular. The gleaming red hair that initially caught everyone's eye was a little shorter now than it had been when she'd been in Congress. Her makeup was light makeup. Her skin, tightened when necessary by the finest cosmetic surgeons available, was flawless. And her body was one of a kind. *Money well spent*, she thought to herself.

Satisfied with what she saw, she smoothed her skirt as she waited for the car that would take her to the twenty-first floor and the apartment of Supreme Court Chief Justice Arnold Mason. He had sounded surprised when she'd called him a week ago and said she had something important to discuss with him. When he'd suggested his office, she had told him she would prefer a more private meeting place. It concerned the presidency, she'd said, and it was urgent.

At first, Mason had objected, saying their meeting would be inappropriate. Jennings replied, correctly, that she currently held no office and was not an announced candidate for any office. This would be a private conversation between two old friends. In truth, they had only met on a few occasions when Jennings was House Speaker. Jennings knew Mason was aware of her reputation for sexual promiscuity; it was common knowledge throughout Washington. She also knew he'd be curious about what was on her mind, so he'd finally agreed, inviting her to his apartment after assuring her that they would be alone and that their conversation would remain private.

As Jennings stepped onto the elevator, she thought of the slim file folder in her purse. Inside was a draft of a proposed Twenty-Eighth Amendment to the Constitution, which called for early elections to replace an acting president chosen by Congress under Article XX, Section 3. The draft had been written and examined by eleven constitutional scholars and was considered legally foolproof. Jennings had slept with three of the men and one of the women who had drafted it, and she was pleased with their product, if not with their sexual efforts.

She had also spent the past three months studying Chief Justice Mason's background and personal habits. Mason's wife, Maureen, had died two years ago of breast cancer at the age of forty-eight. The few times they had met, Jennings had always thought her to be frumpy and humorless, which was exactly how she saw the acting president. Mason was a lonely and still vigorous man, and she had noticed him staring at her on several formal occasions during the previous administration.

She stepped off the elevator, walked up to suite 2134, and knocked on the door.

Mason opened it himself and smiled at her. "Madam Speaker, how nice to see you," he said, motioning her into the room.

"Mr. Chief Justice, it's been too long." Jennings held out her hand and grasped his firmly. She saw his eyes make a quick appraisal of her body. It was what she expected. She didn't want this meeting to be too easy, so she would restrain herself, at least at first. Mason was key to her plans, and she would exert as much sexual pressure as it took to win him over. He was more plain-looking than she remembered and about the same height as her own. His hair was almost completely gray, and he was frequently termed "distinguished" by the press.

Mason led her into his living room and motioned to a plush sofa. "Please make yourself comfortable. And let's drop the formalities, if it's all right with you. My friends call me Arnie."

Jennings sank into the sofa, crossing her perfect legs slowly to give the Chief Justice a good view. "I'm fine with that, Arnie. I'm Lucy." She glanced around the apartment and wasn't surprised at the drab, conservative tastes that had decorated it. Probably the frumpy wife. She promised herself she would redo everything when she moved in. That was all a part of her carefully planned schedule.

He glanced at his bar. "How about a drink? I seem to remember your preference is scotch."

Jennings nodded her agreement, wondering what else he remembered about her. "Yes. Neat, please."

Mason walked over to her with a glass, seating himself in another sofa across from the former Speaker. "So, do you miss being in office, Lucy?"

"Yes. Very much. I miss the—passion—of politics," she said, staring at him. "I like to be involved in using my influence to decide things. Important things."

Justice Mason sipped his drink. "And what have you been working on lately?" He knew this was not a social visit. Jennings wanted something.

Jennings swallowed half of her drink and reached for the file in her purse, placing it on the table between them. "Why don't you take a look at this, Arnie, and then we can talk."

Even more curious now, Mason reached for the file, opened it, and saw only one short page. He sat back on the sofa, and read:

Proposed Twenty-Eighth Amendment to the US Constitution

Section 1: When the Congress shall have declared who shall act as President under Article XX, Section 3, the Congress shall additionally provide for the interim general election of a President as soon as practical but, in no case, no later than two years after the acting President shall have assumed office.

Section 2. The Congress, under Article V, shall propose this Amendment to the Constitution by a joint resolution of two-thirds vote of both Houses. A letter of notification of this proposed Amendment shall then be sent immediately, preferably by electronic means, to each of the several states for ratification by their State Legislatures.

Section 3. Provided however that the several states are not required to wait for official notice of the passing of the joint resolution before taking action. Ratification of this proposed Amendment, under Article V, shall be by Legislatures of three-fourths of the several states. Upon approval, states shall, without delay, initiate procedures to prepare for a general election to elect a President who shall serve until the next regularly scheduled general election.

Section 4. This proposed amendment shall take effect immediately upon approval by the states.

Mason read through the document twice and then placed the single page back in the file, closed it, and returned it to the table. He took a long sip of his drink and looked admiringly at the former Speaker. No way to guess at her real age. Depending on their political persuasion, the pundits estimated her to be anywhere from thirty-five to fifty. She really was lovely, and he wondered at the stories he had heard about her sexual prowess. He had been alone a long time. And he was tired of living a monastic life. Still, he was chief justice of the Supreme Court. No sense making a fool of himself.

"Wow," he said, smiling at her.

Returning his smile, Jennings said, "Is that a legal opinion?"

"Not exactly. My legal opinion is that this—this document—is well drafted. It's brief, to the point, a solid piece of work."

"So you think it would pass muster in the Congress? And more to the point, in the Supreme Court, if it came to that?"

"I didn't say that. And I wouldn't want to be quoted outside of our private conversation here this evening."

Jennings finished the rest of her drink and held out her glass. "May I?"

Mason nodded and took her glass, walked over to the bar, and filled it. His mind was working in ten different directions. What did she want from him and what did it all mean? And what was in it for her?

She couldn't want—could she—the presidency for herself? And how could she make that happen? True, she had wanted to be chosen acting president and, as Speaker, had even passed a previous House bill proposing her name before the last Congress was adjourned. The bill had never been taken up by the Senate and had died when the Congress ended, making the whole thing moot. Then, a radically new and different Congress had been elected, including a House with about an 80 percent turnover in membership, the first such mammoth change in history. Even Jennings had been defeated for reelection in her California district, despite her huge personal wealth from marriages to two multimillionaires.

"So what do you think?" Jennings asked as he handed her the glass.

Mason reseated himself and looked directly at her. "Let's stick with *wow* for the moment. Lucy, everyone in Washington knows you are a brilliant and ambitious woman. How about telling me what's behind all this and what you want from me."

Jennings took another long drink and returned his stare. "It's simple, Arnie. Next week, that proposed Twenty-Eighth Amendment will be submitted to the House and Senate. I'm told that I—we—have enough votes in both Houses to pass it very quickly. It will then be sent to the governors and legislatures of the states. In addition to contacting House and Senate members, my team has had people working in forty-five states for months to assure prompt passage by at least thirty-eight. We are also helping to prepare the states for the coming election." She paused to finish her drink. "We think that somewhere along the way there will be a challenge to the amendment, certainly that woman's—"

"You mean the president," Mason interrupted.

"Yes, a challenge by her legal staff and perhaps by a few others in the Congress. We are also working on the legal aspects of a separate challenge to the election itself. For instance, how will candidates be selected? That challenge will, of course, come to you at the Supreme Court."

"Possibly," Mason replied. "Possibly. The amendment would have to pass Congress first, of course. And then there would be the approval— or not—by the states."

Jennings stood up and walked over to the bar, filling her glass again. "I can assure you, Arnie, that there will be quick passage in Congress. The amendment will then be immediately sent to the states, even if it is also sent to the court. We will not wait for the court's decision, but a preliminary statement of tentative approval from you would speed the process along a great deal." She walked over to Mason and sat down next to him. "We have been working on this ever since the day that woman was appointed."

Mason thought he would be uncomfortable sitting close to her, but he was not. Whatever else she was, she was a remarkably attractive and powerful woman, and he was intrigued and stimulated by her. He kept thinking how long it had been since his late wife, Maureen, had passed away.

"Lucy, you bring up a good point. I'm unclear as to how candidates for president would be selected if this proposed amendment were to pass. If I understand how this would work, there isn't time to conduct a regular campaign. And the Constitution doesn't even mention political parties or candidates."

"We've been working on that, Arnie. I've been in conference with officials of both parties, and they will resolve that problem. Still, the issue of candidate selection is bound to come before you at the court."

"You keep saying 'we,' Lucy. Who else is involved?"

Jennings placed her drink down on the table. "I'd prefer not to use names just yet, Arnie. But you'll find out soon enough. Let me say that strong support will come from the highest levels of two of the three branches of government. And the military. There is intense dissatisfaction with—that woman."

"I wasn't aware it had gone that far. And a preliminary statement from me might be considered unethical to say the least." Mason was being his usual judicious self.

Jennings finished her drink. "Arnie, you know how this town operates and how these things are done. The statement doesn't have to come directly from you. A private word or two by staff around Washington at some cocktail party, and it will cover the city in an hour."

"So, what else do you want from me?"

"I want you to join us—not publicly, of course. You must remain publicly neutral. But you can be immensely helpful in your quiet way. I can promise you that the rewards will be great." She placed her hand in his lap.

Mason had to smile at what he could only think of as the arrogant charm of this woman. She was confident and completely self-assured. And for the first time in years, he felt a desire he thought had been deeply buried.

"I'm tired of talking now, Arnie. Let's see how else we can communicate." She leaned over and kissed him, gently at first and then felt his passion grow, as he groaned and his arms held her closely.

4

"TODAY, MY FRIEND, I WILL show you what the accursed Americans and their allies would give their souls to find—my central headquarters and stronghold."

Bakr and Ali had spent the night traveling from Ali's mud hut on the Syrian border, resting at three separate safe houses and changing vehicles as many times. They had heard aircraft overhead on two occasions, but there was never any contact. Ali was impressed with the ISIS guards, who were extremely protective of their leader.

The two men watched the black SUV they had just left disappear across the dusty desert. They looked out on the desolate land that stretched for miles. Bakr explained they were in the ancient village of Dabiq, just north of Aleppo, in Syria, close to the Turkish border.

Ali knelt down and kissed the ground. "I am honored to be here, my Caliph, where our blessed Prophet Muhammad foresaw the armies of Islam in a final battle against the infidels preceding the end of times. It is here where he told us Islam will triumph over all."

"You know the teachings of our prophet, Ali. Dabiq is exactly why I chose this location. And while it is close to a major city, Aleppo, and to Turkey, it appears to be a deserted village and has no apparent military value. The Americans and even the Russians blast Aleppo with their million-dollar weapons every day, believing they can stop us. And they are so cautious not to violate the Turkish border that they accomplish very little. They never think of Dabiq as being anything but a small, almost deserted village in a barren desert. And we are careful to keep it looking that way.

"That is why we began to construct a massive underground headquarters here over five years ago. Look around, Ali." Bakr gestured with his arms. "What do you see?"

"I see nothing, Caliph. Remnants of a few huts in the village. It looks deserted. There is a pile of rubble over there. Nothing else."

Bakr glanced around. "Let us walk over to that rubble cautiously, my brother, and see what we can see."

As the two men walked, Bakr withdrew from his cloak what looked like a remote control and pressed a silver star at its top. Noiselessly, the largest slab of concrete began to move. It revealed a large, black, metal door. Bakr took out a cell phone and pressed three numbers. Ali could hear metal sliding beneath the black door and voices from below. The door opened inwardly, and four heavily armed soldiers came out. They saluted Bakr, who took Ali by the arm and entered a lighted chamber. The soldiers followed them, closed the door, and pressed a switch that slid heavy, metal reinforcing bars behind it.

Bakr and Ali walked down several steps to another guard standing outside what was obviously an elevator. The guard saluted and opened the elevator door, and the two men stepped inside. Four levels were listed on a panel, and Bakr pressed the button for the first one.

When the elevator opened, four more guards greeted Bakr with salutes as he stepped out. Ali was right behind him but stopped suddenly when he saw what appeared to be an active village, with people moving about and greeting one another. The area was well lit artificially, and children played outside homes. An open marketplace was ahead of them. The black flag of ISIS was prominently displayed everywhere.

"I admire your flag's battle motto, Caliph," Ali said. "*Muhammad is the prophet of God.* While we have all repeated this many times in our daily prayers, it has come to mean much more since I have joined you. With this blessing, you cannot be defeated."

As people recognized Bakr, they bowed and applauded. Those in uniform saluted. He smiled and waved to everyone.

"How do you like it, Ali?"

"It is impressive, Caliph. I, too, had an underground facility beneath my palace in Damascus, but it was nothing as grand as this."

Bakr nodded. "We are supplied daily with fresh food by our own men, as well as by contributions from local farmers. They leave their wares outside remote tunnels at other entrances several miles from here, disguised in much the same way as you have seen above this place. These entrances are heavily fortified and are bombproof, as much as we can make them so. Even a direct hit from the American bomb they call the 'bunker buster' would not harm us. There are three lower levels here, Ali, with even more wonders. In time, I will show them all to you. Come, there is a special event I wish to share with you."

The two men walked to the center of the market square. They entered a building, which had six or seven small rooms with large windows of Plexiglas. Pillows were set up in front of the windows, and Bakr invited Ali to sit in front of one of them. Soldiers were seated on all the other cushions.

"Ali, these are viewing rooms for the women slaves who join us or who are captured by our soldiers. Here the women are inspected by our doctors and sold to the highest bidder. Preferences are given to our soldiers, of course, who are often awarded women at no cost when they have proven their bravery in combat." Bakr clapped his hands, and about a dozen naked women with numbers hanging on cords around their necks were led into the room. Most of them looked quite young. Ali guessed that none was out of her teens.

"You will remember, Ali, that Americans criticize us for making slaves of these women. They do not acknowledge that they, themselves, were a society based on slavery for hundreds of years. Their Christian Bible endorsed slavery, as does our Holy Quran. We have reintroduced many of these old traditions and practices from our holy book. My people have enthusiastically revived this slavery custom of many thousands of years ago. We have found it to be one of our main recruiting tools."

As they watched, two men in white coats, presumably doctors, entered the room and began calling to the women by their numbers. The doctors then inspected the women's teeth, limbs, and private areas. One young woman was pulled out of the line, and a doctor held up a red sign.

"Ah, he has found one of them to be pregnant, Ali. As you know, Sharia law states that a man may not have intercourse with a slave if she is pregnant. This one will either be allowed to give birth in another area or returned to the slave market, or she will be beheaded at a later time."

Ali nodded in agreement.

Bakr turned to two soldiers seated behind him. "Ah, Hamid. As-salaam alaikum. The blessings of the prophet be upon you."

"And upon you as well, Commander of the Faithful."

Hamid's bronze complexion glowed in the lighting of the viewing room. His uniform was neatly pressed and displayed the ISIS insignia on his chest. As with most soldiers Ali had seen, Hamid seemed to be in his late teens or early twenties.

"Hamid, have you chosen any of these slaves to be your own?"

"I have, my Caliph. I am pleased with that number six, despite her apparent youth."

"An excellent choice, Hamid. She has large breasts and a pleasant face and will make a good breeder. Will you please tell my friend Ali our procedures for purchasing these slaves?"

"Of course, Commander. As with all women, the purpose of these slaves is to provide intercourse for us. They will also cook and clean and produce children. This is as the Holy Quran prescribes. Once we take them to our quarters, we find out what religion, if any, they practice. If this religion is not Islam, the Holy Quran encourages that we engage in intercourse with them as soon as possible. If they do practice our religion, this may delay immediate sexual relations, and they may receive better treatment. But they are still slaves."

"Good, good, Hamid. And explain how this intimacy takes place according to the Holy Quran."

"If any slave we have purchased protests her treatment, she is gagged and both hands and arms are bound to the bed. All of us are charged to pray before intercourse because having sex with our slaves is pleasing to Allah, blessings be upon Him. This will provide future soldiers and slaves for your entire caliphate. Sometimes the younger ones will complain about the pain of these relations but an explanation of Sharia law and frequent beatings put a swift end to the complaints."

Bakr showed approval and nodded. "And what happens to these slaves if you or any soldier should die in battle?"

"These slaves belong to each of us. They are our property and can be sold or given by sworn testament to another soldier or to any male family member. We have all prepared these sworn testaments should it be Allah's will that we be taken to heaven on the battlefield."

Bakr turned back to Ali. "This, too, is how slaves were treated by the Americans, Ali. Slaves are clearly the property of the owner and may be passed on after the death of the owner. Thank you, Hamid."

The soldier saluted Bakr, stood, and bowed. Then he left the viewing room to claim the woman he had chosen.

"Your men are well versed in the Holy Quran and in Sharia law, my Caliph. It is pleasing to see and hear them recount the law."

"Yes, Ali. We also teach intensive classes in the Holy Quran and Sharia law. Some of these men come to us with only limited knowledge of our faith. And, of course, some of them from other countries have no familiarity with our religion or culture at all. We find that learning our faith and its teachings gives strength and guidance to our men. I will soon show you one of these classes, my friend, but let us return now to my garden and refresh ourselves with food and drink and pleasant company."

5

GENERAL CLINTON COURIER, CHAIRMAN OF the Joint Chiefs, had just passed his thirty-year anniversary in the marines. Well over six feet tall, Courier weighed exactly what he had on his twenty-fifth birthday. Despite his fifty-seven years, his hair was still naturally jet-black. He kept his body well toned, and his overall health was excellent. His appearance was more than a matter of pride. He was a marine and, throughout his career, had felt he had a duty to demonstrate a personal physical standard to the men he commanded. Now, as head of the Joint Chiefs, he maintained that standard and expected each of the other military chiefs to do the same. This was no affectation for the general. For him, it was a basic principal of leadership.

His Pentagon office reflected his conservative nature. Military insignia of the various units he had commanded were displayed in frames on plain, light green walls. A picture of his late wife was on his desk. He had never had children. His rank allowed him to choose any size office and to decorate it as elaborately and expensively as he wished. Instead, he had chosen one of the smaller offices and had done no redecorating before he'd moved in.

Courier grimaced as he read the latest reports about action against ISIS in the Middle East. Nothing but stalemates or out-and-out losses of territory, equipment, and personnel. ISIS had been successful in mounting major terror attacks on virtually every large European capital, as well as several in Asia and even in smaller towns in the United States.

And the group's recent announcement that Washington, DC, would suffer its wrath had him extremely concerned.

He thought over again his decision to accept Acting President Rose Akron's reappointment to head the Joint Chiefs. After all, he had been accused of threatening a military takeover of the government during the stalemate before Akron had been appointed acting president by the Congress. He still wondered if he would have gone that far. His concern for the stability of the government was somewhat tempered when the acting president asked him to stay on as chairman of the Joint Chiefs. Against his better judgment, he had accepted.

Now, after fifteen months in Akron's administration, he was being blamed almost as much as the president for America's failure to eradicate ISIS. He—Clint Courier—the most awarded and honored Joint Chiefs chairman since Colin Powell, was now being questioned about his military expertise. The whole acting president situation had always seemed to him a lame way to run a government, especially that of the United States. Now, the nation had a woman with no military or governmental experience, and apparently little appreciation for the armed forces as a whole, in charge of a major battle against an ever-growing, extremist military spread throughout the Middle East. And beyond. He felt intensely that this situation had to be corrected.

Courier had now become convinced that a winning strategy—if one existed—had to include American boots on the ground, a term avoided by former Presidents Obama and Danzig and reiterated by Akron. To him, there was no other way. The only viable course of action was all-out warfare and eradication of as much of ISIS as they could find, followed by periodic destruction of smaller cells that would inevitably spring up after the major conflict. There had to be a maximum effort on an ongoing basis for many years, led by the United States. Coalition forces were a joke and could not be counted on. Only the British and French were serious about helping but even they offered only minimal air support and equipment, not armed forces on the ground.

The Israelis had offered their competent and powerful military but had agreed to a limited, secretive role so as not to inflame the Arabic states and give them a reason to support ISIS to a greater degree, as many of them had already. America, Courier felt, should take this step on its own. He planned to make this recommendation to the acting president soon, even before another formal cabinet meeting. If she refused, he would resign and let her deal with the consequences.

What those consequences might be was still an open question. As Courier had reminded President Danzig, both men had taken the same exact oath—"to protect and defend the Constitution of the United States, so help me God." Would Courier attempt a military coup if he felt the Constitution was threatened? It was a question he thought about constantly but, so far, had refused to answer.

As he turned the pages of his latest military status report, he came across a piece of paper that had obviously been copied many times. What was this? A proposed Twenty-Eighth Amendment to the United States Constitution? Was this a bad joke? He buzzed for his aide, Colonel Carter Samuel.

Samuel was quick to respond, knocking briefly on Courier's door and then entering, walking exactly three steps away from his boss's desk, and saluting.

"Sir?"

Courier, returning the salute, held out the single page he had just read. "Cart, what's this shit?"

Samuel glanced at the sheet. "Sir, this was received in the mail this morning, addressed to you, anonymously, of course. I thought you should see it."

"What for? This is bullshit, and you know it. It might take years for something like this to be approved by the states, and Akron will be gone by then."

Samuel remained at attention. "Sir, I remind the general that legislation was passed a few months ago in almost all states to speed the process of state approval of any future constitutional amendments. It is now possible for approval in a matter of weeks—actually sooner—if state legislatures so choose. Voting is all done by new shielded computers, using voice and fingerprint identification."

Courier looked up at his aide, a man who had been with him in Afghanistan, Iraq, and Syria. "I know all about that shit, Cart. I liked the improvement from a military perspective. But this proposed amendment ... This feels like it has Lucy Jennings behind it, doesn't it?"

"Yes, sir. Word around Washington is that her organizations in over forty states have lobbied state legislatures to take up the matter immediately after it has passed Congress. Apparently, she has unlimited resources."

Courier grunted. "She approached me on this subject a few months ago, and I told her she was nuts."

Samuel grinned. "Crazy like a fox, sir."

"That may be, Cart. I can't see how she would be an improvement over the person we have in office right now. At least our current president hasn't slept with every man, and quite a few women, in Washington." Courier knew this was only a slight exaggeration. "Besides, the Supreme Court will probably squash the whole thing."

"Yes, sir. Unless she's been able to reach Justice Mason."

Courier's look hardened. "You think there's a chance of that?"

"That's the word on the street, General."

"Good God Almighty, I never would have thought that Arnie Mason would—

"Cart, get me an appointment with Mason as soon as possible and keep me apprised of the progress of this situation."

"Yes, sir. Latest word is that this proposal will be introduced in the House and Senate this week. I am told that passage is assured."

"Keep on it, Cart. I'll be goddamned if I'm going to take orders from another woman president."

6

BAKR AND ALI SIPPED TEA and lay back on soft, fragrant pillows in the garden of Bakr's underground headquarters. Ali marveled again at the surroundings. Luxurious, yes, but not too ornate for a caliph. Spacious, well-lighted rooms with tall, red walls held paintings, separated by Arabic scimitars, of devout religious figures from Middle Eastern history. One wall displayed more modern weapons; another, a row of world and regional maps. And still another showed prominent verses from the Holy Quran. A large, red, mahogany table with matching chairs was used for battle planning with Bakr's commanders at least once a week. Several species of Middle Eastern birds were suspended in golden cages throughout the gardens. Multicolored parrots were allowed to move freely around the area. Heavily armed guards were posted at all corners of the villa. Up above them could be heard the distant sounds of war.

Two stunning American women had just left them. The women—both teenagers—had begged to join ISIS and were quickly taken to Bakr for his personal enjoyment. The men shared the women, who were energetic and eager to please.

"I hope you are now able to relax, my brother," Bakr said to Ali. "I assure you it is quite safe here. The Americans think our main headquarters are farther to the east and north in Raqqa. The truth is that Raqqa has never been our capital. We keep changing our military locations every few weeks or more often if needed. It is easy to outwit them and the other infidels. They think their expensive aircraft with radar that can penetrate the ground can find us. But we have protective shields above us that keep us safe."

Ali agreed. "Yes, Caliph, this is an ideal location. The young women were excellent. I always preferred American whores. They are so willing to demonstrate their … devotion." Ali leaned back on his pillows. "While I have read about the holy village of Dabiq, it is such an honor to be so close to where Muhammad himself actually walked. And from a military standpoint, with your proximity to the Turkish border, you can make a quick retreat if you are attacked."

Bakr grinned and shook his head. "The new Islamic State never retreats, my brother. And this holy place has never been attacked. You spoke the other day of the end of times, showing your deep reading and belief in our Holy Quran. Allah, bless him above all others, has protected us. We have believers imbedded even in the military of the infidels, so we are informed of the timing and locations of their attacks. Of course, occasionally we allow some of our minor forces to be captured or even destroyed so that the Americans believe they are making progress." He laughed loudly. "Later, I will show you more of our underground facilities where our men work tirelessly toward our ultimate goal."

Ali nodded. "I am already impressed with what I have seen, Caliph. But I have many questions."

"And they will all be answered. What can I tell you?"

Ali considered. "It is hard to realize that we are underground now, my brother. This is so beautiful. Tell me, do you also keep your planes and missiles down here, below the surface?"

Bakr stood and walked to a large map of the Middle East. "We have no need of these kinds of weapons. They are expensive and have failed us in the past. They are also easily located by our enemies. Our new weapons are biological and even atomic. Our scientists are working even now on the latest techniques for perfecting them."

"Atomic you say? And biological?" Ali was impressed. Before the recent war, his people had begun work on poison gas and atomic armaments, which he planned to launch atop his missiles. But his scientists were not able to finish them in time, and the missiles were ineffective as well. "You speak of poison gas, my brother?" Ali stood to join the caliph.

"No. Well beyond gas. Far, far beyond." Bakr stroked his beard as the two men walked around the garden. "You are familiar perhaps with viruses?"

"You mean such as the Ebola plague that was consuming Africa? What of it?"

"The Ebola virus is the deadliest ever known to man," Bakr said. "Once it spreads, it is virtually impossible to stop. In the past, the virus could only be transmitted by direct contact with the blood or body fluids of an infected person, or by touching the body itself. Now, French, American, British, Chinese, and Indian scientists in our laboratories have found a way to keep the virus active for almost two weeks in the very air we breathe, as well as for a more limited time in standing water and food. They are about to complete a process that will enable mosquitoes to carry and transmit the perfected virus. This deadly virus is virtually unstoppable. Its mortality rate is over 90 percent. And we have made it even more powerful."

Ali showed his surprise. "You have the hated Americans and their accursed infidel friends working for you? How can this be?"

Bakr walked over to his new friend and embraced him. "It is proof that Allah, blessings be upon him, is with us. We have volunteers from more than ninety countries, Ali. They come to us willingly, and they are begging to die for us—men and women, along with their children. Can you guess how many we number now?"

"From what you have described, you must have at least ten thousand, Caliph."

"The Americans say we are twenty thousand. But, as usual, they are wrong. We are more than fifty thousand, Ali, and we exist throughout the world—most heavily in Europe, Africa, and Asia, but also in virtually every country, including the accursed United States itself. Our people appear to be very ordinary and behave as good citizens in all countries.

"They will do so until we release them to strike and destroy the infidels, as has already happened in cities large and small throughout the pagan world. We have reached the point now in the United States where people who are not even a formal part of ISIS are attacking schools, churches, and businesses in our name. These are small attacks, but it has made the Americans fearful and distrustful of their leaders."

Ali was amazed. Fifty thousand? No missiles or aircraft? Laboratories filled with Ebola virus? How had this man accomplished so much in so short a time? Perhaps he was truly a prophet.

Bakr spoke with enthusiasm. His voice became stronger with every statement. "For a hundred years, we have been the lap dogs of the Americans and the West. The Crusade-inspired wars of their own making desecrated our countries in the Middle East during the First World War. Then they divided our states to suit their own whims. At first, they wanted our oil, and we took their money. Then, the infidels found their own oil resources and did not need us as much as before. They began to create disturbances throughout all the Middle East with the obvious intention of hoping we would destroy ourselves. That was their big mistake."

Bakr turned to Ali. "The Americans are weak and stupid. They depend on their vast military to control us, but military might means very little today. Real power is in biological weapons and computers and in controlling the press and what they call social media. We have mastered all of these. The Americans think they have identified us and our locations. They call us—what is that English word—nicknames, like ISIS and ISIL and Dash. The more of these names they create, the more comfortable they feel. Their media love this game too. Their news and Internet broadcasts only serve as recruitment tools for us. Our enemies are truly ignorant, and they will pay for their ignorance, God willing."

Ali did not know if this strange man was a blessed gift from Allah or totally insane. "But, surely Caliph, we cannot defeat the Americans and their allies solely by using this Ebola you speak of. Their military weapons are still strong."

Bakr's eyes held a strange gleam. "Ebola is not the only virus our scientists have been working on, Ali. Have you ever heard of the Marburg virus?"

Ali shook his head.

"It was derived from African monkeys in the 1960s by German scientists who worked for Hitler during the Second World War. I have studied this man Hitler, Ali. He united his people when they had been torn apart by the infidels after the first war. This is not unlike what I am achieving now. Hitler did not accomplish this unity by offering sex and drugs and entertainment as the Americans do. He offered his people struggle, danger, and death. He declared Germany the Aryan master race and told the world that we in the Middle East were the original Aryans. Then, he almost single-handedly defeated the accursed Americans and English in the Second World War. I offer our people the same hardships and glory as this man Hitler, with a greater reward after death, Islamic heaven. That is why they follow me."

Ali considered this. "And this Marburg virus you mentioned. Tell me more about it."

"Certainly, Ali. It is similar to Ebola but attacks the nervous system in slightly different ways. This virus, too, we have perfected to keep it alive in air and water and food. Its mortality rate is 80 percent. And there is even more. Our scientists have also devised a method to adapt and intensify the centuries-old bubonic plague to add a third element to our plans for a viral epidemic. This plague has a mortality rate of over 90 percent if it is not treated. The men we have working on these viruses have changed their compositions so that there is no prevention or cure for any of our mutated viruses. We are only weeks away from being able to combine all three viruses and having them at our disposal. And I have not yet told you of our compact but potent atomic weapons."

Bakr walked toward a map of the United States.

"Now we come to the final solution, Ali, my friend. This is another phrase I have borrowed from the man Hitler, who also despised the Jews. First, we will weaken and cripple our enemies in their own countries with the release of a combination of these fortified viruses. These same germs will also be distributed to countries all over the populated world in two waves, aimed first at their military and their governments. As one wave's strength begins to wane, we will release another. Our scientists estimate that, in two or three short weeks, we can weaken, if not destroy, 80 percent of their military. Their population will die even more swiftly. They have no vaccination or antidote to our modified viruses. The germs cannot be treated with current drugs. The deaths of their people will be slow and agonizing. They will not be able to respond, except to beg for mercy."

"Surely you do not plan to defeat them completely only through the use of these viruses?"

"No. I plan only to weaken them so they cannot defend themselves."

"And what then, Caliph?"

Bakr walked toward a podium in the garden and mounted it slowly. "Then, Ali, my brother, when the infidels are weakened and on their knees, we will release our atomic weapons. The fires of hell will consume the world, as foretold in the Holy Quran. In their crippled conditions, they will be unable to oppose us. At that moment, I will be revealed as the Mahdi, here to lead all faithful Muslims in the end of times, God willing." He raised his arms to the sky, and his voice echoed throughout the garden.

Ali was stunned. He was, of course, familiar with the end times belief as told in the Holy Quran. The Mahdi would reveal himself from the city of Dabiq, and the world would be consumed with cleansing fire. Only the faithful would survive, and from them, the Mahdi would create a new world ruled by Islam. This man Bakr truly believed he was a prophet and the Mahdi spoken about in the Holy Quran!

"And, this cleansing will be brought about through your atomic weapons, Caliph?"

"Yes, our ultimate weapon is being completed as we speak. As the ignorant Americans and Russians continue to work on costly, larger rockets and bombs, a team of atomic scientists from Iran, North Korea, Pakistan, and other countries has developed a new range of lightweight, portable atomic devices that are simple to transport and easy to set into motion. With the new shielding developed in our laboratories, they cannot be detected. So, as the world is already on its knees from the viruses I have described, I will call for the conflagration. Atomic weapons in every capital of every country that opposes us will all be detonated at the same moment. The Earth will go up in flames. Everything will be cleansed through fire as it says in the holy book, and only our brothers in Islam will survive!" Bakr began to weep, but his face lighted up as he spoke.

"Then—only then—when the corrupt and sacrilegious peoples of mankind have been destroyed, will those of us who have been selected to remain begin again—all followers of Islam and our beloved prophet, bless his holy name. The world will be ours, Ali. *Ours alone!*"

Bakr was silent for a time. Ali considered what he had heard. How had this man accomplished so much in so short a time? Was he inspired, touched by Allah himself? Even blessed? Could it be that he was truly what he claimed?

"Caliph, excuse my ignorance. I am fascinated and impressed by what you tell me. How did you come to learn so much about the Americans and other westerners? Have you lived in their countries?"

Bakr stepped down from the podium and walked over to Ali. "It is the Americans themselves who taught me about their weapons and tactics while I was their prisoner."

Ali could not conceal his shock. "You were their prisoner? Allah, blessing be upon him, must have been watching over you."

Bakr nodded. "It is only through his divine guidance and inspiration that I survived and was able to lead our people to so many successes. I will tell you tonight about that captivity and my rebirth. But now, let us refresh ourselves as we approach our time for prayer."

7

SENATE MAJORITY LEADER TOM FALKNER laughed as he reread the Proposed amendment to the Constitution. It was as former Speaker Lucy Jennings had said it would be—a foolproof, perfectly constitutional way to rid themselves of the current acting president. That woman was really something.

A tall, handsome man, Falkner was only fifty-five and kept himself in good physical condition. He still had solid support in the Senate and among those who had previously voted for him. Falkner had been married and divorced twice and was narrowly defeated in the last presidential election. But his desire for the office had never waned. He had been looking for a way to get himself back in the discussion for the presidency but had decided to just let things run their course until the next regular election. This proposed amendment might be just what he needed.

He and Jennings had discussed the matter thoroughly, if you can call having exhaustive sex over a long weekend a discussion. Falkner knew that Jennings wanted more than anything to be president, and he believed that developing the amendment would assure her of that outcome. She needed him to support the movement in the Senate, after the amendment was introduced in the House. That placed him in an excellent position to accomplish two things. First, he demanded that Jennings give him a written pledge that he would be her vice presidential selection once the proposed amendment was passed and the process began to elect an interim president. While Jennings felt confident she would be the choice of her party to run for president, Falkner had other plans.

What she didn't know was that Falkner had no desire to be vice president and intended to maneuver himself into being his party's nominee for the presidency at the proper time. He was a member of the party committee, and that might mean he would have to recuse himself when they voted. But he could still lobby them beforehand. He knew he had good support in the Senate and much of the House. After all, hadn't he come in a close second in the last regular presidential election? Bedding Jennings had been a bonus, as far as he was concerned, although who'd bedded who and for what reasons was an open question. And between the sheets, she was as good as advertised.

Picking up his private cell phone, he pressed the name of House Speaker Dante Caruso of Florida. To assure Falkner's support for the presidency, he would promise the vice presidency to Caruso, a man he knew had no future ambitions. It would also guarantee Falkner strong Hispanic support for the next regularly scheduled election. God, he loved Washington's political intrigue!

"Hello, Dante? How are things going in the people's House? Good, good. Do you have time for some lunch in my office this afternoon? I have something important to both of us to talk about. Good, good. This will be completely private; no staffers present. I'll see you around noon. Thank you, Mr. Speaker."

8

VICE PRESIDENT CARSON DANSBY HAD served quietly as a senator from New Mexico for three terms. When his two grown sons had married Hispanic women in his state and had several children, he'd displayed them all prominently at every campaign stop when running for reelection. He had been considered unbeatable. He looked at the pictures on his desk. His son Jack looked a lot like him—dark skin, wavy, blond hair. Dansby wanted him to run for office, but politics was not his major interest.

He had been surprised when Acting President Rose Akron had called and asked him to accept the vice presidency after her appointment by the Congress. He was, he realized, a safe choice for Akron. She had some support in the House but almost none in the Senate. He was respected in that body; had his name on several pieces of important legislation; had never been involved in any scandal; and, more to the point, had no enemies. He could help her there when she needed it.

Dansby read the proposed amendment with little interest. Once the acting president was no longer in office, by whatever means, he wondered what his role would be. There was no mention of the vice president in the amendment. Traditionally, when a president left office, the vice president did too. Whatever the procedure, Dansby knew his usefulness would be over, and he intended to retire to his ranch in New Mexico. He had never enjoyed Washington politics and had no further ambitions. He was content fulfilling his major, and some said only real duty, as Senate president, presiding over that body. Still, he wanted to be completely loyal to the acting president.

To her credit, Akron had kept him thoroughly involved in every important matter in her administration. He felt like a full partner. But he knew former Speaker Lucy Jennings wanted the office and that she had been working for months on a way to gain it. The proposed amendment might just pull it off.

Dansby sighed and reread the proposed amendment. *Well-drafted*, he thought. If Jennings had done her homework, and he felt certain she had, it would probably pass both Houses very quickly. While President Akron had not made many friends in the Senate, she had lost most of her previous House support too. He knew that Senate Majority Leader Tom Falkner still had presidential ambitions, so he would not help Akron's cause. The main complaint about her was that she appeared to be timid and had done so little. Sometimes, Dansby knew, this was the best course for a new president, especially the first one in history to be chosen by the Congress and not by a vote of the people.

Still, if she wanted to remain in office, she needed a major personal victory of some kind. There was no domestic issue he felt could bring that about. The battle against Islamic extremists was the most important item on America's agenda. A major commitment to declare an all-out fight against ISIS could be what she needed. The big question was whether or not that was what she wanted. After all, she had been drafted into the presidency by an extreme quirk of fate. Well, perhaps he could be helpful to her as one of his last duties before he left office.

9

MOSHE RABIN, CHIEF OF THE general staff of the Israeli armed forces, was puzzled. As he viewed the latest satellite photographs of key ISIS positions throughout the Middle East, he could easily see a dozen or more opportunities for targets the allies could attack and destroy. And yet, the Americans continued to ignore most of these key objectives. It made no sense to him. He would call his friend General Clint Courier, with whom he shared all ISIS information, and encourage him to take action. Surely, Courier must already be able to see with American satellites what Rabin could see with his own. Perhaps it was the American president who held Courier back. But why? For every day—for every hour—they waited, ISIS grew stronger. His own military analysts believed that a major attack was being planned by these Islamic radicals, most likely against the United States. Courier must also know this.

But what really concerned Rabin were vague reports from Israeli spies within the ISIS ranks suggesting new secret weapons research was almost complete. What were these weapons? Previous information from American sources had given him names of biological scientists from several countries, including the United States, who had been working with ISIS for over a year on top secret projects. Gas? Germs? Although he needed more detailed information, it was very dangerous to try and contact the few Israeli agents imbedded within ISIS. There had been leaks, of course, but they were very nonspecific. And escape from ISIS was practically impossible. It had been tried several times with little success.

He was already aware of ISIS research into atomic weaponry, but he knew they did not have the necessary missiles or other assets to launch such weapons. Rabin realized the time was near for a critical change in the long-standing Israeli pledge to stay out of the war against ISIS in an active capacity. After all, his country was as threatened as all the rest. Perhaps more. These ISIS forces hated the nation of Israel even more than the other Arab nations who had been trying to destroy his country since its modern beginnings in 1948. He would discuss his feelings with Israeli Prime Minister Ehud Shamir this afternoon. He reached for his phone to make the call.

10

"GENERAL, IT'S ALWAYS GOOD TO see you." Arnie Mason shook Clint Courier's hand and offered him a chair in his private Supreme Court office. "I assume you're not here because someone has threatened to do away with the military." It was an old joke the two men had used before.

"Not this time, Arnie. And I wish I had some better humor to share with you."

Mason's smile faded. "I see. Well, how can I help?"

"I have two things on my mind that prompted this visit. First and foremost, I don't think I have to take a lot of time to tell you that things are worsening in the Middle East and that we have done little to turn the situation around. Even our allies have expressed increasing concern about our lack of leadership and aggressiveness. I've advised the president about these matters and, of course, she has seen the reports and satellite images. Frankly, I'm very worried."

Mason thought for a moment. "Clint, the only knowledge I have of the situation is what I read in the papers and see on television. But, that's enough to understand your reactions. I'm sure you've emphasized the deteriorating military situation to the president."

Courier grunted. "You can bet your ass I have, for all the good it has done me. And others on the Joint Chiefs have echoed my feelings, as have the British, French, and Israelis." He paused and took a deep breath. "Arnie, I'm afraid the problem may be that the president means well but has absolutely no background in the way government or the military works. She certainly doesn't know how to fight a war."

"That's understandable, given her history before she was chosen for the office."

"And I get that. We all do. The real question is, how long do we wait until the situation gets so grave—even urgent—that responsible people must take action?"

Mason was troubled by Courier's serious tone. "Clint, can I get you some coffee?"

The general shook his head.

"So, are you here for my advice or just to get things off your mind?"

"Neither. Arnie, I think we're very close to deciding what we in the military must do to protect America and the Constitution. I know that the oath you took when you were sworn in is very similar to the one I made—to support and defend the Constitution against all enemies. To be clear, I'm asking where you would stand if the military decided to—well, let's say, take charge of the war."

Mason was shocked. He had known Clint Courier for over twenty years, and knew the general was a loyal American who had come close to giving his life for his country on many occasions. He had never heard him speak this way before and realized Courier was desperately serious.

"Clint, I don't know what to say. It sounds like you are considering a military takeover of our government."

"Arnie, you know me pretty well. I'm not interested in overthrowing the government. I'm no dictator. I want to beat—to destroy—ISIS before they get any stronger. Our window of opportunity is closing quickly. I want to approach the president about personally managing the war. That's all."

"And what if she refuses?"

"Then we'll have to make other plans. We just can't let things drag on like this."

Mason straightened up in his chair. "General, I have to say that I cannot and will not condone a military takeover of the United States under any circumstances, if that is what you are suggesting."

"Even if the current administration's conduct of the war threatens our national security and the Constitution?"

"Even then."

The two men stared at each other grimly.

"Mr. Chief Justice, I have another concern that may be related."

"We may as well get it all out, General. Go ahead."

Courier cleared his throat. "Mr. Chief Justice, it's come to my attention that you have formed a ... eh ... personal relationship with former House Speaker Lucy Jennings. I also know that she has drafted a proposed constitutional amendment that would require an interim election for president, effectively removing Rose Akron from office."

Mason's face turned bright red. He stood up. "General, you are entirely out of order. My personal life is none of your business, and I'm going to ask you to leave my office."

Courier stood and faced Mason. "I will in a moment, and I'll make this brief. Arnie, if all of the things we've discussed this morning come to a head and involve both of us in a very personal way, I hope you can maintain a proper perspective on the most serious legal matters that may have ever come before the Supreme Court in its history." The general turned and left the office.

Mason's mind was racing. He had no problem with people knowing about his relationship with Lucy Jennings. It was impossible to keep a secret in Washington anyway. In fact, the relationship had swollen his ego to a great extent. He'd never believed that he could attract a woman like Lucy, and he had become obsessed with her. What really bothered him about what Courier had said wasn't just the possibility of a military takeover but that his connection to Lucy might become a part of it. As much as he was in love with Lucy, his dedication to the Supreme Court had always come first in his life.

11

T HE LOVELY AMERICAN GIRL RAN her fingertip beside the blade of the golden sword as her right hand caressed the body of Abdul Anwar Ali.

"Tell me something, my dear. How is it that you came to our country and the caliphate?" Ali slowly caressed the woman's breasts.

"I wanted to see if the power was real—the feeling of power." She continued to stroke his sword.

"You like power?"

"Oh, yes," she said, climbing on top of Ali. "Yes. Yes. Yes." She threw her head back and screamed as she climaxed.

Abu Bakr entered the room. "You are all right, my brother? I thought you might have killed the girl because she displeased you."

Ali threw the woman to the side. "No, Caliph. Not at all. She is perhaps too quick, but she is young and will learn."

"Of course. Tomorrow you must try the new French girl who arrived a few days ago from Paris. She is sixteen, no longer a child, and has many skills. And she is not—how do you say it—too quick."

The two men laughed as the woman left the room.

"Caliph, you promised you would tell me about your time with the Americans and what you learned. I am most anxious to hear your story."

Bakr seated himself on cushions next to Ali. He clapped his hands, and two beautiful, naked Arabic women entered the room with a tray of hot tea, set it next to the two men, and left quickly.

"First, let me explain to you what the Americans and the West have never understood about the Middle East and its people. We have been ruled for thousands of years by strong, even cruel men. Never a woman. Women, as you know, are for bearing children, cooking, and lying down when men desire them. Once again, the cursed Americans have proven their stupidity and vulnerability by choosing a woman for their president. She knows little of politics or the military. She has no strengths. For centuries, the justice of our rulers was always swift and often cruel. They did not care if their people loved them as long as they feared them. And we never hesitated to send men into battle, even against enormous odds.

"We have never had a need for this democracy that the Americans seem to love and admire so much. An American general said it well when he told the world, 'There are no Thomas Jeffersons in the Middle East.' Strength and belief in power and the Holy Quran are what attracts young people from all over the world to us, my brother. We are strong and have compelling beliefs in Islam and the Holy Quran. They are our guides. We do not waste time trying to understand these young people who join us or their feelings; they must understand us. Obey us. Die for us. And they will all willingly do this. Or they know they will be publicly beheaded or set ablaze.

"How did I learn this? It was during what the Americans call the Second Gulf War—when the United States came illegally into Iraq and forced our brother Saddam to flee. I was a soldier fighting to protect the homeland and was captured by the infidels and placed in Camp Bucca. You have heard of this place?"

Ali nodded. "It is most infamous, my Caliph. Many of our brothers were tortured and killed there."

"Yes. But it was there I began to realize how stupid these Americans truly are. Our brothers were disorganized, and some had lost their faith. The Americans, in their ignorance, merged us into one group—the most infamous and cruel of all of the various fighting factions of Al-Qaeda and other Islamic units. From them, I learned a great deal.

"It was easy to become friends with the Americans who ran the camp. They are so gullible. After I had been tortured for a few weeks, I told them how I loved freedom and the story of America. In time, they believed in and trusted me. I could speak many of our dialects and was chosen to translate for the Americans. Of course, I told the infidels only what they wanted to hear, revealing nothing important. Their biggest problem in the camp was that the prisoners were constantly plotting, fighting, and killing each other."

Bakr sipped his tea, an odd smile on his face. "I used this incessant upheaval to prove I was a lover of peace. I began to teach classes in the Holy Quran. This was like a blessing from Allah. In a short time, the fighting groups became more peaceful, and the Americans became more trusting. I, too, began to feel a deeper understanding and to draw strength from our holy book.

"I had permission to walk among my brother prisoners at night, holding the Holy Quran, under the guise of continuing my instruction. And all this time, I was forming a new strategy that would become the Islamic State." Bakr became very serious. "I can share this only with you, my brother. One night, as I was walking between tents in the camp, I was blinded by a bright light—a vision from the Prophet Muhammad, blessings be upon him. He told me I was to head this new state. He promised it would gradually take over the entire Middle East and then the world." Bakr's eyes began to glow.

"I learned well from the infidels and from my brother prisoners. I can tell you that, if there had been no Camp Bucca, there would be no ISIS. Bucca was an ideological factory. It helped me construct the caliphate as we now know it. We have the Americans to thank for all of this. In fact, one can say truthfully that, without the Iraq War and prisons like Camp Bucca, ISIS would not have been born."

Ali listened in amazement. That such a momentous blessing should arise from a cursed existence in a prison—only Allah himself could have brought this about.

"How do you rule this caliphate, my brother?"

"I do not rule. I lead. We rule ourselves under Sharia law as described in the Holy Quran. We do not hesitate to punish and kill when necessary and we reward those who deserve it. We share our victories and our defeats, as well as our food and women. We have pledged our lives to one another."

Ali thought on these things. "Caliph, I asked the American woman why she came to join you, and she said it was power that attracted her."

Bakr nodded. "Yes, as I said before, these young men and women, especially the Americans, have lost all the discipline in their lives. They had no direction, nothing to believe in. They took drugs and fought against their parents and their governments. They trusted no one. They became fascinated with television news pictures of ISIS, our beheadings, and our attractive young people who invited them to join through their media. ISIS became their hope, their golden dream. They flocked to us by the hundreds and then by the thousands. Many brought money. All they wished was to serve and fight and give their lives. The more we beat them, the more they clung to us. The more they saw the beheadings and castrations we used against our enemies, the more they loved us."

"This is amazing, my Caliph. Truly you are blessed. Truly ISIS is blessed. And you have accomplished this in so short a time and with ordinary weapons."

"This is true," Bakr said. "Our most important and dangerous weapon, my brother, is the discipline within the Holy Quran. These young Americans are used to the *turn-the-other-cheek* beliefs in the Christian Bible and their other so-called holy books. Only the Holy Quran teaches them the peace that comes with power, discipline, and victory through the death of infidels. This is how we have been winning and how we will continue to do so until the end of times. ISIS is an ongoing revolution, Ali. It has become a holy fighting machine powered by prayer and devotion to Allah. It is our destiny to take over and rule the world."

12

NABIL SAWALHA, CHIEF OF THE Arab League, sat as his desk in his luxurious office in Cairo. He was frustrated. Formed in 1945, the League was impressive on paper but, in reality, was powerless and inept. Sawalha opened his gold-encrusted League membership volume. It showed membership of twenty-two Arab countries, which contributed over $129 million annually to maintain a Joint Arab Military Force of more than forty thousand so-called elite troops.

None of this was true.

Only twelve Arab countries maintained a membership and paid dues. There was no Joint Arab Military Force to speak of. If it were not for his own country, Egypt, the strongest of the Arab nations, and Saudi Arabia, the League would not even exist on paper. And this was all the fault of no one else but the Arab nations themselves. They agreed on only two points—avoid conflict of any kind and, above all, hatred of the Jews.

There was a phrase in the founding documents of the League, which was often repeated by members at their irregular meetings—Arabs do not kill Arabs.

With rare exceptions during the League's seventy-five year existence, this phrase was strictly adhered to. The exceptions often amused Western nations but they made perfect sense to most Arabs.

The League often stated that it had only two enemies—the hated Israelis, of course, and the equally hated country of Iran, which was Persian, not Arabic. What truly guided all Arab nations and their Muslim citizens was that the peoples of these Arabic countries were composed of two sects, the majority Sunni and the often-persecuted Shia. There were a half dozen other, smaller sects, but they were unimportant.

For thousands of years, Sunni Muslims had contented themselves with purging and murdering Shia Muslims in Arab nations. Technically, this violated their pledge that Arabs do not kill Arabs. But they simply ignored the pledge and made exceptions. It was easy to hate, if not attack, Iran. Their people were predominantly Shia Muslims. So in Iran the Shia Muslims persecuted and murdered the minority Sunni. Arabs had, in fact, been killing other Arabs for over five thousand years.

Westerners were often confused by these pledges and sects and thousands of years of Arab history. It all made no sense to them. But, for Arabs, this was always easily understood and accepted. However, things were vastly different now. ISIS had shaken these time-honored Arab prejudices and traditions to their core, and that was why Nabil Sawalha was frustrated.

He looked over a request from the United Nations that the Joint Arab Military Force take up arms against ISIS, which now existed in great strength in all Arab countries and throughout the world. This was a first in the history of the United Nations, which had always understood that the Arab League was ineffective and that its military never took up arms against anyone. Individual Arab countries would occasionally deal with local uprisings themselves, but not the entire Arab League.

Truly, the ISIS problem had changed all the traditional rules. ISIS was composed of Arabs, Europeans, Asians, and Americans, Muslim and infidel alike. They recognized no sects. Their publicly stated goal was to take over the entire Middle East. Recently, Sawalha had come to believe that the secret ISIS goal was much, much larger.

It was a global goal. It was to absorb everyone, everywhere. True, ISIS wanted to convert all people to Islam, a noble objective, but surely, Sawalha thought, not at the cost of destroying all governments in all countries, especially those in the Arab world.

When the Arab nations first became aware of ISIS, they felt the group was just another offshoot of Arab splinter organizations that had always existed under different names. Their main purpose was to harass the West and kill Israelis. So most Arab countries contributed generously to ISIS. But something had happened to ISIS under its mesmerizing leader Abu Bakr. ISIS forces murdered everyone who disagreed with them, Arab and infidel alike. This man, Bakr, who called himself a caliph, would not sit down with Arab leaders and listen to their careful explanation of thousands of years of Arab history. This meant nothing to Bakr. He would rule the Middle East and then the world in his own way and time, he told them.

And he had grown so powerful so quickly that Sawalha felt it was time to do the unthinkable. He would call a meeting of the Arab League and ask for a vote to declare war against ISIS.

13

HOUSE SPEAKER DANTE CARUSO SEATED himself comfortably in the black, leather chair next to Senate Majority Leader Tom Falkner. He looked around the luxurious office, noting the many plaques and awards Falkner had gained over the years. Caruso was proud that he had risen from a small immigrant Cuban family in Miami to become Speaker. And now he was sitting in the same room as a man who had almost been elected president two years ago.

"Dante—may I call you Dante?—I know you've heard rumors of a proposed constitutional amendment, which would call for an interim election of a president to replace an acting president appointed by Congress, as we have now."

"Yes, Senator. And I received a copy of the amendment just yesterday. It is ... interesting to say the least."

Falkner nodded in agreement. "Indeed. And we both know this has been instigated by former Speaker Lucy Jennings. She has always wanted to be president and thinks this is her easiest path."

Caruso frowned. "I served in the House under Jennings, but I was never part of her team. It always seemed to me that her interests were often not those of the people. And her personal ... uh ... character left a lot to be desired."

Falkner laughed. "I know exactly what you mean, Dante. You'd think that, after Bill Clinton's mistakes, Congress would have learned a thing or two about promiscuity."

Caterers arrived, set lunches before the two leaders, and left the office.

"Let's eat while we talk. Dante, I've been doing a little private polling and have become convinced that, if this amendment is agreed to by the states, it should not be a forgone conclusion—a coronation if you will—for Lucy Jennings. There are several potential candidates who would make excellent presidents."

"I agree, Senator. And I must say that your name should be foremost among them."

Falkner was very pleased. This would be easier than he thought.

"That's kind of you to say, Dante, and I am still interested in the office. With your help in the House to introduce and pass the amendment and send it to the Senate promptly, perhaps we can begin the process while I organize a campaign." In truth, Falkner had kept his previous organization and a massive war chest intact from his first run for president. "And I also want to ask you a personal favor."

"Of course, Senator. What can I do?"

Falkner put on his most earnest look. "Should I receive the party's nomination, I would like you to seriously consider running with me as my vice president."

Caruso was stunned. He'd had no expectation of anything like this happening in his political life. He'd thought he would eventually run for the Senate but never for any higher office.

"Senator, I'm ... well ... overwhelmed. And speechless. I would be honored, of course."

Falkner reached across the table and shook hands with the Speaker. "I'd like to keep this confidential for a time while the process evolves, Dante. I know you can understand."

"I understand completely, Senator. I'll get things moving promptly in the House. I can promise you that. The proposed amendment will be introduced tomorrow. And you have my appreciation and complete support."

14

WALLACE HUTTON HAD BEEN DIRECTOR of the *Federal Register* for seventeen years. While many of his duties were quite mundane, he was most proud of being in charge of processing proposed constitutional amendments on behalf of the Archivist of the United States, his immediate superior. After all, it was not every federal employee whose job was authorized by Article V of the Constitution.

Hutton had a master's degree in library science. He lived alone in a small apartment in Washington and had never married. His position as director of the *Federal Register* was his whole life, and he took all of his duties quite seriously. Hutton had never met President Rose Akron; he had never met any president. But he felt she was doing a good job under very stressful circumstances.

Like many other people in Washington recently, he had received a copy of the proposed amendment. Staffers he knew in the House and Senate were saying that it would pass both chambers very quickly. Hutton had no opinion about the amendment; it was simply his job to make certain it was drafted and signed properly and sent speedily to the governors of each of the fifty states. At that point, his duties were over until the governors notified him as to whether or not the proposed amendment had been approved or rejected by their state legislatures. If at least thirty-eight states approved, Hutton would draft a formal proclamation for his superior, the archivist, to certify that the amendment was valid and was now a part of the Constitution. He would then publish the certification in the Federal Register. While this would be Congress's official notice that the amendment process was complete, he knew that they, and the entire nation, would know the result almost immediately. CNN and the other networks would make certain of that.

Hutton thought it odd that the president was not involved in this process, but it was not his job to question the procedure—only to make certain that all legal steps were followed to completion. Because he had been told that Congress would take up the matter very soon, he began working on preliminary measures that would speed the process once he was notified. Foremost among them was checking on the correct and safe computer transmission of the proposed amendment to the governors. This would be the first time in history a proposed amendment would have been sent to the states in this manner. Hutton keenly felt the pressure of this responsibility. It was entirely possible that the government of the United States would change because he had pushed one small computer key.

He and his staff had drafted policies and directions for the transmission, including instructions to the governors for sending notification back to Hutton. To make certain every state received the official proposed amendment, Hutton had decided to transmit the document both by encrypted e-mail and fax. He had e-mail addresses and fax numbers for the governor's office in each state. His transmission would be preceded by a test message explaining the process and asking the governors to contact his office if they had not received the document by a certain date and time. He was determined that the operation would come off flawlessly. After all, one could say that the entire fate of the nation would be in his hands.

15

"GOD DAMN IT, BOBBY, THERE'S nothing about parties mentioned in the Constitution. They didn't even exist when the country was formed." Jimmy Brickell had been chairman of the Republican Party for three years. He had agreed to sit down with his Democrat counterpart to decide how candidates would be selected if the proposed constitutional amendment was passed and sent to the states.

"Jim, all I'm saying is that we have had parties in this country for hundreds of years, and in recent history, candidates have been chosen by primary and caucus voters in every state and, ultimately, by the delegates to our conventions." Party Chairman Robert Stanford was concerned about the whole amendment process disintegrating into a horrible political mess.

"There isn't time for that in this special election, Bobby. So I'm suggesting that both of our parties take control of the situation, choose our best candidate, and let the election decide who becomes president."

Stanford was appalled. "So what you're saying is that you and I are going to sit in some smoke-filled room and decide who our next president will be." He threw his legal pad across the room.

"That's the way it used to be done; you know damn well that both parties handled it that way in the past." Brickell replied, picking up the pad and sliding it back across the table to Stanford.

"We'll be sued for certain."

"Sued for what? There is no law that states we must have primary votes to choose candidates. And under the circumstances, we really have no choice. There is simply not enough time. Here's what I propose, with the understanding that our own organizations can do whatever they damn well please. Each of our national committees has about fourteen members, give or take a few. So, we call them together for the purpose of drafting a candidate with a firm deadline for selection. That's the person we nominate."

"But both of our committees have members who are in the House and Senate and may want to be candidates themselves. What do we do about that?" Stanford could see disaster coming.

"People on our committees who want to run for president are simply ineligible to vote. That doesn't mean they won't be chosen, just that they cannot cast a vote. And they can choose to run themselves even if the committee doesn't select them. No law says they can't." Brickell was taking the path of least resistance.

"This is going to blow up in our faces, Jim. What if one or both of our committees aren't able to choose a candidate?"

"That makes the whole process much easier, Bob. We'll only have one candidate running for president, and the suspense will be over!"

Again the legal pad was thrown, this time directly at Brickell. "I'll be goddamned if that's going to happen to my party. Whoever we choose will beat the hell out of your candidate."

Brickell started laughing. "Well, we'll know before too long, won't we? And what if our Acting President Rose Akron decides to run? After all, she's only been president for fifteen or sixteen months."

"The national party makes the choice whether she likes it or not."

"Spoken like a man who is about to lose his job," Brickell said. "By the way, when do our committees meet?"

"Any time now, buddy. Any time now."

16

HOUSE SPEAKER DANTE CARUSO RAPPED his gavel loudly. "The gentlewoman from Texas has called for the vote on House Bill 77, the proposed Twenty-Eighth Amendment to the Constitution. We have debated this amendment for two hours. The gentleman from Ohio has suggested the absence of a quorum. All members will indicate their presence."

Caruso was simply following usual House procedure. He had the votes to pass the proposal but wanted as many yes votes as possible. The quorum call would bring all members not already present into the chamber. There was great interest in the amendment, and most members were already seated. In a few minutes he was ready.

"A quorum being present, members will now cast their votes, yea or nay, for the proposed amendment."

The electronic voting board lit up quickly. The total—425 yea votes, 8 nays, and 2 abstentions. It was a dramatic endorsement of a method to elect an interim president until the next regularly scheduled election.

"The clerk will immediately send House Bill 77 to the Senate for its action. The House stands adjourned," Caruso said, smiling.

17

VICE PRESIDENT CARSON DANSBY LOVED the Senate he had served in for eighteen years. As he entered the chamber, old friends left their seats to greet him. Dansby was a rarity, in that he had not made any enemies during his three terms. He was a gentleman at all times, listened carefully to debates, and voted based on his genuine beliefs about the merits of a bill. Or if his party had good reasons for him to vote a certain way, he would follow the party dictates in that case. They could always count on Carson Dansby, the senior senator from New Mexico. The fact that he had never authored a controversial bill in all his years of service was another reason he was universally liked.

His Senate colleagues had been surprised when he'd accepted Acting President Akron's request that he join her administration as vice president. He explained privately that he had decided to retire after his current term ended. He did not have a big ego, appreciated the support he'd always received from his constituents, and would have been content to retire to his ranch near Santa Fe and live out the rest of his life with his charming wife, Kyla. Her family owned a highly successful wine distillery in the state, and they would live very comfortably.

All of his friends said they understood, but many of them had objected to Rose Akron when she was chosen for acting president, and her confirmation vote had been very close in the Senate. Still, their friendship with Dansby had ensured his overwhelming confirmation as vice president.

One of the most vocal in opposing Akron as acting president was Tom Falkner, who had narrowly lost the previous presidential race. Although outwardly friendly toward Dansby, Falkner remained angry over Akron's selection and objected to any business her administration brought to the floor of the Senate. Carson Dansby was unaware of any of this when, as a courtesy, he called Falkner's office for an appointment. Falkner greeted him at his office door.

"Mr. Vice President, you know you don't need an appointment to see me." Falkner's voice was easygoing and cordial as he shook hands with Dansby. "After all, you are president of the Senate."

Dansby smiled and accepted a seat on the sofa next to Falkner. "A position with only one duty, Tom, as you well know. I have to say, you haven't given me much of a chance to use my limited power over the past year and a half."

"Carson, we can set up a tie vote for you any time you would like one."

The two men laughed and talked over old times and old friends for several minutes.

"Tom, I know you're busy and I won't keep you. I'm here to discuss this proposed Twenty-Eighth Amendment that calls for an interim election."

Falkner's smile dimmed somewhat. "Certainly, Carson. I think we've just received it from the House, and I intended to vote on it today. Is there any problem?"

"Tom, first let me explain that I'm here on my own and not at the president's request. I don't think she'd approve of my visit. As you know, my primary duty as vice president is supporting the president in any way I can. There hasn't been much I could do for her so far. My only experience has been in the Senate, and I thought I might be helpful here."

Falkner nodded. "I see. How can I help?"

Dansby considered his approach. He didn't want to annoy Falkner; he simply hoped to reach some kind of understanding with him that would give the president more time—more breathing room—as she tackled the many problems she had before her, especially the ISIS situation.

"Tom, you know how much I respect the Senate and its traditions and rules."

"Of course, Carson. No one is more admired for the way he handled himself in the Senate than you are."

"Thanks for saying that. I just don't want you to feel that I'm out of order. It's clear that this proposed amendment, if it passes and is approved by the states, would end the president's term abruptly. It seems to me that it wouldn't give her a fair chance to solve the problems she faces. I guess you could say that asking for fairness is really why I'm here."

Falkner wanted to let Dansby down gently without insulting him. "Carson, normally I wouldn't hesitate to help you if I could. But the fact is that the Senate is overwhelmingly supportive of the amendment. I think the feeling is that the president has had a year and a half or so to deal with the domestic and foreign problems, and she hasn't shown us very much. In fact, almost nothing.

"Now, I'm not saying that she hasn't tried and that she isn't sincere. And I'd be the first one to say it isn't her fault. She came from nowhere to the House during that disruptive election two years ago, and then she finds herself elected Speaker and then chosen as President. That would blow anyone's mind, especially someone with no governmental experience at all. Carson, the feeling in the Senate and in the House and in much of the country is that we need a change—a big change."

Dansby could tell from Falkner's expression and tone that he had no chance to change his mind. He knew there was a lot of truth in what Falkner was telling him. Still, he felt obligated to make one more try for the president.

"Tom, I appreciate what you're saying. Perhaps if you could see your way clear to delaying the vote on the amendment so that the president would have a little more time, that might prove beneficial for all of us."

Falkner sighed. "Carson, I wish I could do that, but there's no sentiment for it. The president just doesn't have a lot of friends around here. She's even lost many of them in the House. I wish I could do what you're asking just on the basis of our own friendship. Certainly, I could delay a vote for a day or two. But what good would that do?" Falkner shrugged his shoulders.

"You couldn't give us as much as a month then?"

"I'm afraid not, Carson. It just won't fly."

"Well, I won't keep you from your duties any longer, Tom. I do appreciate your taking time to hear me out. Thanks."

"Thank you for the visit, Mr. Vice President." Falkner's voice and smile were bright and cheerful again. "You know you're welcome back home in the Senate any time."

The two men shook hands, and the Vice President left. He went back to the Senate floor to say hello to a few more friends and then walked slowly out to his office, Secret Service agents following closely. He had learned a great deal about internal political dealings in Washington after being a politician in the town for most of his adult life. This gave him a keen insight as to what could happen in this situation. First, Rose Akron was in real trouble and would probably lose the presidency when the amendment was passed by the states. Second, Dansby felt Tom Falkner wasn't as innocent as he appeared. He still wanted the presidency and had probably already made moves in that direction. In fact, the proposed amendment may have been his own idea, although Dansby had heard it was the work of Lucy Jennings. Finally, he could best serve President Akron by supporting her decisions and backing her up in every way possible.

18

"NINETY-SEVEN YEA VOTES IN THE Senate? Really?" Acting President Rose Akron shook her head as she turned off her office television. "Sherm, what the hell is going on in this country? And why is this thing moving so quickly?"

Sherman Boyle looked at the report in his lap. "Damned if I know, Madam President. Do you want to hear the rest of it?"

"Sure, why not," she said, pushing her chair back and standing up.

"The proposed amendment has already been transmitted to the states for approval. Or rejection."

"Ha. What rejection? Anything else?"

"Now we wait."

Akron walked around her desk, sat down across from Boyle, and poured them both some coffee. "Realistically, how long might it take for approval?"

Boyle thanked her for the cup and sipped a little. "With all the publicity about the amendment and the instant news society we live in today, most of the state legislatures have already been called into immediate session. They only need a simple majority to pass the damn thing. And over forty of the states have approved voting by computer for their legislatures now that there are ironclad safeguards. As I mentioned before, the amendment needs thirty-eight state approvals. Our latest polling says they could conceivably get that many in a day or two."

Akron laid her head back on the sofa and exhaled. "Then what?"

"What do you mean?"

"I understand that once the director of the *Federal Register* receives thirty-eight approvals and publishes the results, the amendment becomes law. So we have a Twenty-Eighth Amendment to the Constitution that requires an interim election for president. How does that happen? I mean, how do the parties and states physically make that happen? I'm not completely clear on this, but doesn't each state have a method for choosing a candidate for president? That used to take a year or two. We have—or had—a process in place that required campaigning, caucusing, and state primaries. Then conventions and nominations, and finally, election day."

"Madam President, you're right when you say 'used to take a year or two.' The two major national parties feel the amendment will pass quickly, and they'll announce today that they will select a candidate for the presidency within ten days by a simple majority vote of their national boards. Parties are not controlled by Congress. They're not even mentioned in the Constitution. So the parties can do anything they decide to do."

"But, can't that be challenged legally?"

"Sure. Anything can be challenged. And I expect it will be. Certainly in the Supreme Court. And I'm certain the court will expedite its decision or just decide not to hear the case. Obviously, there are bound to be more questions before the court, in addition to those from candidates chosen by the parties. For instance, what about other individuals who want to run for president? I think that's where the first challenge will be."

The president put her coffee cup down sharply on the table. "You know, this sounds like a science-fiction movie."

"A bad one, I agree."

"Okay, then what about Election Day? Do we just wait until November?"

"Our attorneys say Congress will have to step in here and set a new date. My guess is that it will be shortly after the announcement of the two candidates by the parties. I've seen a draft of another bill that will set a new election date thirty days after the passage of the amendment."

"Thirty days? That's ridiculous. How can anyone campaign for the presidency in just thirty days?"

"I agree that it's unrealistic. And there are already rumors that the thirty-day thing will be challenged in the Supreme Court. They really have no role in this, but that's never stopped them before. Ultimately, Congress will probably have to pass a new law extending the date."

"I appreciate the way you've stayed on top of this," Akron said. "Just for the sake of argument, Sherm, what would happen if I, as the acting president, presented my own legal challenge to the court?"

Boyle almost spilled his coffee. "Your own challenge? What kind of challenge? I mean, what would you challenge?"

"I haven't made up my mind yet. But I'm not going to just sit here calmly while my administration collapses."

19

ISRAELI PRIME MINISTER EHUD SHAMIR sighed deeply as he looked at his most trusted friends. Across from him sat Moshe Rabin, chief of the Israeli armed forces and Yitzhak Shavit, chief of the Israeli Security Agency, almost never known by its full name, the Institute for Intelligence and Special Operations. Shavit reported directly to the prime minister.

"Gentlemen, this is a conversation I hoped we would never have. The two of you have come to me with irrefutable evidence that ISIS has possession of monstrous new biological weapons—viruses you say—never before developed, for which there are no antidotes or cures. As if this wasn't enough, you also say they are close to completing development of lightweight, portable atomic weapons powerful enough to contaminate, if not destroy, the capitals and major cities of most nations with any military power. We know this is not far-fetched because we, ourselves, have been working on such devices. Am I understanding you correctly?"

Both men nodded.

"Mr. Prime Minister, as you know, we have been fortunate to infiltrate the lower ranks of ISIS for several years," Rabin said. "The latest reports from our men and women in ISIS are detailed and frightening, as you have seen, and were obtained only through great effort and loss of life. Fortunately, one or two were able to escape to Jordan with their information. Some of what we relayed to you is rumor, some gossip, and some reality. We had to decide what is real and what is fiction. We believe the truth is that there is no question that ISIS is about to launch attacks. Their plan is to use the biologics in a first wave. That will be followed by some form of nuclear attack. We don't know how or when."

"I agree, Prime Minister," Shavit said. "It is only a question of time. And limited time at that. The virus germs, by the way, are almost ready for use. ISIS is working day and night on completing the atomic weaponry. This type of device is more complicated and sensitive, of course, so it is taking longer. We know the number of mechanisms exceed fifty so far. Our people tell us each of their atomic weapons can generate a blast of approximately 10 kilotons. As a comparison, the Hiroshima bomb was about 15 kilotons. We can thank modern science for this ability to miniaturize hellacious weapons of this kind."

"But why do they need both weapons—the biological and atomic—for their attack? You'd think only one should be enough to get our attention."

The other two men glanced at each other.

Rabin chose to speak first. "This is the most difficult part, Prime Minister. Our intelligence is that they—"

"There is no question about this, Prime Minister," Shavit interrupted.

"Yes, yes. Go on."

"Our intelligence is that they intend to release these new biological weapons first in all the major capitals. Our people believe this will be done in air and food—even water." Rabin stopped for a moment.

"Continue, Rabin."

"We also think they can transmit these viruses through insects. Flying insects."

The prime minister was shocked. "Insects? How can this be? Our own scientists have told us this is impossible."

Rabin indicated his agreement. "Apparently that is no longer true, Prime Minister. Times change. Science progresses. And ISIS has many good scientists working on this problem, including some Jews. We have always known that viruses can change and adapt on their own, over time. ISIS has found a way to speed up that process. Regardless of how they are transmitted, the viruses have a life cycle of at least two weeks under normal circumstances. Strong winds and rain can affect them, of course. Still, it is estimated there will be an 80 to 90 percent death toll. Then, after perhaps ten days to two weeks, ISIS will detonate the nuclear devices."

All three men were silent.

"And ... and ... they can truly do these things?" the prime minister asked in disbelief.

"Oh, yes sir. Without question."

"But, but, if your figures are correct, this could have the effect of destroying most of the civilized world. What could they possibly gain?"

Rabin again. "Sir, their leader, Abu Bakr, believes he is the chosen one, the Mahdi described in the Quran's apocalypse or end of times. He believes it is his destiny to destroy the world through fire. And that he will survive. Our Torah also tells of an apocalypse, of course, as does the Christian Bible."

The prime minister pounded his desk. "But this is insane. Even if he has protection against the biologicals he releases—"

"No, he does not. There is no antidote and no protection." Shavit said this without passion. "I know this is hard to believe, sir."

"Hard? It's damn near impossible. And after the biological, he will set off the nuclear devices?"

"Exactly."

"He is obviously a madman. How will he survive?"

"He believes he is Allah's divine messenger and that he will survive all of these weapons, along with enough of his followers to create a new world"—Shavit stumbled, stunned at his own words—"a new Islamic world where all nonbelievers have been destroyed. He and his survivors will then rule a worldwide Islamic state of peace."

Again the three men were silent.

"And you expect me to repeat this incredible story to the Americans?"

"Prime Minister, we had the same doubts you are feeling when we first heard of these things. But the evidence has made us believers."

Another minute passed. "And you say that our people in Jordan who gave us this information cannot tell us where they escaped from?"

"Unfortunately, that is correct, Prime Minister. When they were captured, they were blindfolded and brought to this base or camp. They escaped at night and were lost in the desert for weeks. It is a miracle they are still alive."

The prime minister considered what he had heard. "All right, gentlemen. I will make the call to the American president, who only thinks she has trouble now with this so-called special election. Wait till she hears what I have to say. What is your best estimate of how much time we have before we must act?"

Rabin looked at Shavit and then turned to the prime minister. "Perhaps a month at the most. I think sooner."

"All right. When I can set up the call, I would like you both with me. I will ask the American president to also have your counterparts available. Of course, you already know this means a war that could easily ignite the entire planet, at the end of which there will be no winners. There may be no one left at all. Thank God our agents have uncovered this plan. I am reminded, Shavit, of Mossad's motto. 'For by wise guidance you can wage your war.'"

20

NABIL SAWALHA RAPPED HIS GAVEL again and looked over the twenty-one delegates to this emergency meeting of the Arab League. The delegate from Syria was not present. Rumors were that he had been killed in a recent attack by rebels on the Syrian capital.

"My brothers," Sawalha declared, "the blessings of Allah be upon you for agreeing to meet together this morning. I know you will all join me in thanking the government of Egypt for hosting this meeting and providing the usual amenities. As you know, we are here because of a request from the United Nations that the Arab League commit its forces to the fight against ISIS in our brother countries. This is the first request of its kind from the UN in our history. The floor is open for discussion. I recognize the delegate from Saudi Arabia, King Muhammad Al Saud, custodian and protector of the two holy mosques and a strong shield for Allah, may his name be praised."

King Muhammad was one of fifteen thousand members of the Al Saud family and had ruled his nation for twelve years. While in his late seventies, his mind was still sharp, and he was noted for guiding his country and most of the Middle East through many crises over the years. He was dressed in traditional Arab garb, his beard long and well trimmed.

"My brothers. Blessings be upon you and your families. I bring you greetings from my family and my entire nation. I know that many of you have urgent business in your own countries and it is to your credit that you have taken time to discuss this—how can I call it—this ill-timed and unwarranted request from the American-controlled, so-called United Nations. I will keep my remarks as brief as possible, God willing. We all have our own feelings about this ISIS movement and its leader Abu Bakr. Indeed, I must say that most of us in this room have contributed monetarily and militarily to this man, who, among other pronouncements, has sworn to crush and annihilate the hated Zionists in Israel."

Loud applause filled the room.

"True, he has entered some of our lands and conscripted many of our people into his armies. We in Saudi Arabia, like all of you, have registered our complaints with Bakr and received concessions from him. I have been particularly pleased that, in addition to his successes against the Zionists, he has also frustrated and defeated the Americans and other Western nations who continue to invade our countries under the guise of creating one of their democracies and what they believe will be a lasting peace."

More applause, including several delegates pounding their desks.

"The West has continued to divide and upset the natural order of things in what they call the Middle East for well over a hundred years. In the past, we could do little to prevent their illegal and immoral tactics. They wanted our oil, and we needed their money. Now they want less oil, and we no longer need their cursed dollars."

Delegates now stood in unison, applauding and shouting.

"This man Bakr, by whatever name his organization may be known, has kept his promise to defeat our enemies and restore Islam to its proper place in our own countries and eventually around the world. He is not our enemy. The hated Jews and the West—they are our enemies. I say we should not only refuse this request from the UN but also send our refusal back to them soaked in pig's blood. *May Allah be praised!*"

The room erupted in shouting and applause. Swords were drawn and waved. Delegates gave loud thanks to Allah, all of this for more than ten minutes.

When the room had returned to order, Sawalha, who had bowed to King Muhammad and shaken his hand, lightly wrapped his gavel.

"I join you all in your appreciation and support for our brother King Muhammad's remarks. Are there any others who wish to speak?"

The Egyptian delegate, General Amman Labib, also dressed entirely in traditional Arab garments with no military insignia, walked to the front of the room. Labib was the latest general to rule Egypt after a military coup.

"I echo all of the words of King Muhammad, especially his suggestion for sending back our reply to the UN. Egypt will no longer support the interference by the West, especially the Americans, who think they know better than we do how to rule our countries and worship our God, Allah the most high."

Delegates applauded once again.

"While I do not wish to keep any of my brothers from speaking, I would like to move that we immediately send our unanimous rejection to the United Nations and adjourn this meeting, so that we can get back to the serious business of ruling our countries." General Labib returned to his seat.

The delegates applauded and shouted approval. There was no strict parliamentary system for administering meetings and votes of the Arab League. Delegates usually followed the lead of Saudi Arabia and Egypt, and both countries had clearly expressed their wishes.

Sawalha wrapped his gavel softly. "I see it is the clear desire of the League to reject the request of the United Nations. If there are no further remarks, I will respond as you wish to the United Nations." Sawalha waited for a few seconds and then wrapped his gavel again.

"This meeting is adjourned. General Labib invites you to remain for afternoon prayers, some refreshments, entertainment, and pleasant company."

Several delegates applauded at this announcement, remembering past encounters with beautiful women and sumptuous feasts. Sawalha sighed deeply. *Some things will never change*, he thought, *God willing.*

21

SUPREME COURT JUSTICE ARNIE MASON watched Lucy Jennings, transfixed. She had raised his level of passion far beyond where it had ever been before. She was a wonder, and he smiled up at her. Jennings seldom expressed joy in any way. Right now, she was hard at work, making certain Mason was thoroughly and completely exhausted. And certainly satisfied.

Finally, he was able to relax and breathe deeply and was ready to drift off to sleep. She lay beside him quietly for a moment. But this was no time for sleep. She needed him alert and responsive.

"Arnie, I need you awake." She shook him, reminding herself that she needn't work so hard on him in the future. At first unsure of himself, he'd soon become quite easy for her to manipulate. And, although she had originally thought his devotion was amusing, Jennings had no further need for amusement. After all, this was business.

"Arnie, listen closely. This is important. I need your strict attention."

"Lucy, you know I always listen to you."

"Fine. Tomorrow, I want you to call a private meeting with the other members of the court. The subject will be the recent petitions to the court asking for hearings challenging the new amendment to the Constitution—a ridiculous attempt, I might add—and an even more problematic legal suit asking the court to both delay the special election and allow for additional presidential candidates to announce they are running."

Mason no longer worried himself with the ethics of his personal situation. He was infatuated with Jennings and would do anything to please her. "You do understand that I can't force them to vote any certain way, Lucy?"

"Of course, Arnie. I'm *not* stupid. Just do what you can. My private attorneys tell me it's a cinch the court will allow other candidates; it's fifty-fifty about a delay in the election."

Mason looked admiringly at her perfect body. He wished he was more aggressive with her and could match her own intensity and passion, but he could not. He had started taking a male enhancement prescribed by his doctor, but it was not doing much for him. He kept telling Jennings that he would do better. Her only reply was that it wasn't necessary.

"My own personal feeling is that your attorneys are probably right on both counts. I'll do my best. And the court may not even have to act. As you know, we can simply refuse to hear any of these requests."

Jennings watched Mason's worshipping look. He was such a child. His sexual needs were meager compared to what she was used to with others. He responded to her every touch and whim. She knew he would do whatever she asked.

"I'm counting on you, Arnie," she said. "I know you won't let me down."

22

GENERAL CLINT COURIER LOOKED CAREFULLY at the faces of the Joint Chiefs sitting with him in his private cabin on Lake Liberty in Maryland, just across the border from Washington, DC. With him were his vice chairman and the heads of the army, navy, air force, marines, and coast guard. Despite his lofty title as chairman, Courier had no direct command of any military forces. He was the senior adviser to the president, or in this case the acting president. But the five heads of the military did command their various services, and he knew he would need them. He had asked for this private meeting, explaining that this would be a "boys only" fishing weekend. None of these men were fools; they all realized something more important was on Courier's mind.

Their suspicions were increased when Courier announced he wanted them to leave their phones and other electronic devices at home or in their offices. Before they arrived, he had his own staff sweep the cabin and grounds for recording devices and remote transmitters. There were none.

These men had known and trusted each other for twenty years or more. Several had been in combat together in Iraq, Afghanistan, or Syria. They were intensely loyal to Courier, and their military records were unblemished.

"Gentlemen, I know you've all been waiting for me to tell you what's really on my mind. And it's not that I didn't catch the most fish over the past few days."

There was polite laughter as the group waited.

"Look. I'm not going to throw a lot of 'rah-rah' shit at you about duty, honor, and country," he continued. "You're all loyal Americans and the best our military can produce, or you wouldn't have the ranks and responsibilities you have. I want to talk to you this morning about the obvious crisis we have with the weak leadership in our government and its failure to act decisively in the Middle East.

"That situation, as you know, has reached dire proportions. ISIS continues to grow, become stronger, and even prosper. The little we are allowed to do to oppose them has been wholly ineffective." Courier paused and poured himself some water. He was a total abstainer from alcohol.

"So far, I've been telling you what you already know. Now, here's what you may not know. Our friend Moshe Rabin called me late last week. He was quite upset. They have several of their people imbedded within ISIS, something we have been unable to accomplish. These men and women have discovered ISIS strategic plans that may well destroy most of the known nations on this planet. I can't go into detail here but their prime minister is calling Acting President Akron to set up a meeting to discuss the situation." He paused again until he was sure he had all eyes on his.

"Gentlemen, I think the time for discussion is over. In fact, we have little or no time to move forward to protect our country, which we are all sworn to do. Our acting president is a fine woman, but she has absolutely no understanding about military matters. And, in this dire situation, I'm afraid she is at a total loss. In addition, she has rejected my suggestions and counsel, as well as those from other strategic thinkers within the military and civilian communities. I've come to the realization that we must act swiftly and surely to take charge of our military and confront this catastrophic turn of events before ISIS can enact their plan. I know that you must have questions, so I'm going to stop now and answer them as best I can."

There was a long silence. Finally, Air Force General Chuck Clark cleared his throat. He was the senior member of the Joint Chiefs and

Courier's closest friend. "Clint, can you tell us more precisely what you have in mind and how you intend to go about taking action?"

Courier nodded. "Chuck, I intend to protect this country from disaster no matter what I have to do—no matter what it takes. The conference call with the Israelis takes place tomorrow. You will all be present. We'll know more when we hear and see the acting president's reaction to the full briefing. Then I can tell you what I intend to do. In the meantime, I think it would be wise to bring your forces under full alert. You can call it a practice exercise and make certain the president is aware of what you're doing."

General Corbin "Cort" Timmons stood up. "Clint, I'd like a straight answer from you, man to man. Are you talking about a military takeover of the United States?" He sat down abruptly.

"I'll give it to you simply, Cort. If that's what it takes to protect and save our nation, that's what I'll do. I don't want to do it, but I feel we've waited too long as it is. Obviously, I can't do it without all of you working with me and standing by my side."

Timmons looked at his fellow officers and frowned. "Clint, this nation has faced a lot of crises since it became a country. There's been talk of military takeovers during all of our world wars. We all know that we may have come close to an assumption of power by the military during the Civil War and in the Cuban Missile Crisis. I can't speak for anyone but myself, but I'd be hard-pressed to go along with a—well, let's call it what it is—with a coup. I'm just being honest."

"I appreciate that, Cort. Is there anyone else who feels the same way?"

The men looked at each other steadily. No one spoke.

"Good. Cort, I know that none of us feels anything but respect for you. You may change your mind after the conference call with the Israelis. We'll have one final meeting soon after the call is completed. Until then, I expect our discussion to remain confidential."

23

BAKR AND ALI HAD BEEN studying maps of the Middle East all morning. Bakr shared previously confidential information with his friend concerning the placement of ISIS forces throughout the region. Ali was astonished not only at the total number of troops involved, but also at how much territory ISIS had gained is such a short amount of time.

"I congratulate you, Caliph, on your planning and operational expertise over the past few years. You have created a fighting force to rival any in the world."

"I thank you, Ali. It is only with Allah's guidance that this has been accomplished. But enough of studying these maps for the moment. You are in for an exciting experience this morning. It is a momentous time for our people. I want you to see one of the most secret underground areas."

Bakr led Ali down a corridor leading to a doorway Ali knew opened onto the underground village of Dabiq. As the two men drew closer to the town's center, Ali saw a large, metal cage with two obvious prisoners. A crowd had gathered close to the scene and applauded as they saw Bakr approach.

"These men are known to be Jewish agents, Ali, and have been spying on us and our facilities for several months. They are about to be executed. It may be interesting to you to know that we have several Jewish defectors from Israel who informed on these traitors. We usually keep the Jews away from secretive areas, but these two had important scientific knowledge we felt would help us. We will not make that mistake again."

Bakr waved his arm, and four soldiers began spraying the men in the cages with a liquid, which, from the smell, was some petroleum product, probably gasoline. When the prisoners were thoroughly soaked, the soldiers turned to Bakr, who again waved his arm. The soldiers lighted torches and threw them into the cages. Both prisoners were instantly engulfed in flames. Their bodies writhed in the fire, but neither man made any sound. The crowd again began to applaud. The stench of burning flesh was everywhere.

"This is what happens to hated Zionists who try to infiltrate and inform on us," Bakr yelled loudly. "Tell everyone you meet what you have seen today. It is the ultimate penalty. Remember that there is no law but Sharia law and no justice but Sharia justice. Now I invite you all to see what else happens to traitors, blasphemers, and infidels. Come."

Bakr gestured to the crowd, which quickly followed his lead to another part of the village. Here, Ali saw about a dozen men kneeling down before an open pit. Several of them were praying loudly; others were moaning and crying.

"My people," Bakr cried out. "Look before you at these serpents, those who have betrayed the caliphate and all of you. They have been tried before a Sharia court and found guilty of crimes against Islam. They are here to be executed."

At Bakr's signal, three soldiers advanced with drawn swords. Bakr gave another sign, and the three men walked slowly down the line of those kneeling and swung their swords. In a few minutes, all of the prisoners were executed, their heads lying in the pit below them.

"This is what Sharia justice means, my people. Keep this vision in your minds and hearts. There is no God but God, and Allah is our God."

Bakr and Ali turned away from the execution site and walked slowly back toward Bakr's quarters. Once inside, Bakr led them to an elevator and pressed the button.

"What I have seen is most impressive, my Caliph," Ali said. "Your men are well trained. Would that all cowards and pigs received the same treatment, God willing."

"Ah, soon your wish will come true, Ali. You are about to see exactly how we will bring that about."

"Caliph, do our people know how much information the two Jews were able to steal from us and if they were able to communicate it to Jerusalem?"

Bakr nodded. "We know they were able to gain some understanding of what we were working on and may have been able to convey that to their Zionist bosses. We are still trying to determine how they transmitted their information. The Jews are deceptive and cunning, Ali. Some have been able to escape. But whatever they were able to learn, they did not know the timing or totality of our attack plans. Only I possess that knowledge. In a few weeks, perhaps sooner, what they knew will be of no importance."

As the elevator door opened, he and Ali stepped inside with two guards and descended slowly.

"When you see what awaits you, Ali, you will be as surprised as our Western enemies. After I put our initial plans together, I decided we would need the most intelligent scientists from all nations and the very latest computer techniques and equipment. I worried about having enough money to finance such a global operation. But Allah, in his holy wisdom, provided everything. Selling the oil we appropriated as a tax from our neighbors provided millions upon millions. Then others began to send us donations, some out of fear, others because they believed in our cause. It took time, but in the Middle East, time has always been a friend to us. Now, Ali, we receive two to three million a day—*a day*, Ali! These millions have financed and continue to pay for all you see here.

"While the West, especially the Americans, have concentrated on bigger and more expensive weapons, to the point where they are bankrupting their countries, we decided years ago to develop only in two areas, as I have already told you—extremely potent viruses and small, portable atomic devices. No rockets, no aircraft, and no tanks and other costly hardware. When we need them for battle, we simply take them from the cowardly, so-called American allies like the Iraqis. When we sense that the West needs a victory to brag about, we allow the infidels to capture a few of our troops. Many of these men are also cowards we leave behind because they could not stand the rigors of fighting for ISIS."

The elevator began to slow and finally came to a stop. As they stepped out, Ali could see the corridors of the vast underground ISIS laboratories he had heard so much about. The size of the facility was much more elaborate and detailed than he had ever imagined. Hundreds of men of every nationality—no female workers were allowed here—performed intricate tasks with machinery of all types. Many were tightly focused on computers. Others dressed entirely in white, wore surgical masks, and worked behind steel walls with small, insulated windows. There was no talk, no idle chatter.

"We are almost ready, Ali," Bakr said. "Several more weeks at the most; perhaps much less. And then the attack begins. The men behind those walls"—he gestured as they walked—"are making certain the atomic devices are perfected, a most difficult task. The formulation of the various plague viruses is complete and ready to be delivered by our people to strategic locations around the world. I have brought you here today not only to see the laboratories but also to witness the testing of these viruses."

Ali had seen many weapons laboratories of his own in past years but nothing like this. Every man kept to his task and paused only briefly for a quick bow toward Bakr as he passed by.

"Testing, my Caliph? Surely, these viruses have been tested many times before."

"Of course, my friend, of course. But only on animals of all kinds. We saved the tests on humans until a short time ago. We know these viruses can kill swiftly and painfully. But *how* quickly on humans is still a question."

Bakr gestured toward a small door on their left guarded by four huge men in checkered kaffiyehs, or head cloths, in different colors, signifying the man's country or region of origin. Ali recognized they each held Russian Special Forces APS assault rifles. ISIS actually possessed more American rifles and other weapons recovered in battle but preferred the more reliable Russian counterparts. The men came to attention as Bakr and Ali approached and then opened the door for their leader and commander.

Inside, another vast laboratory appeared, staffed by more men dressed in white. They worked in and around a smaller room, perhaps ten by ten, with what looked like Plexiglas walls allowing a full view. There were smaller compartments atop the room. Several men were working on these, placing aluminum canisters inside the compartments.

Bakr guided Ali into a waiting room adjoining the larger laboratory and gestured at some comfortable-looking cushions. The two men seated themselves, and Ali watched curiously as two beautiful young Western women were brought into the small Plexiglas room. Neither woman struggled; both of them held hands with their escorts. The men left, and the women seated themselves on soft cushions.

"Why do they not struggle, my Caliph?" Ali asked. "Surely, they must know they are going to die. And from the descriptions you have given me, their deaths will be agonizingly painful. Perhaps they have been drugged?"

"We do not force anyone, Ali. And no drugs or alcohol are ever allowed in any ISIS facility or used by our men. These are, after all, forbidden by the Holy Quran. If we find any who violate this rule, they are immediately executed. Our people all know that we work for rewards that will come later, in heaven, as promised in the scriptures. These women have performed useful services for us. Now, they are more than willing to give their lives for our mission. You may remember the one with golden hair was with us several nights ago."

Ali nodded. "Yes, yes, I thought she looked familiar. She was pleasantly aggressive with me. I remember complimenting her."

"Watch now, Ali. The canisters contain a mixture of the three viruses I described to you. They have been altered and perfected by our leading biologic scientists. They are far superior to their original strains and, as I said, can survive in most environments for long periods, with some exceptions for heavy rain or wind. Let us see what these killer viruses can do."

The men working on top of the room with the young women made some slight adjustments with their equipment and climbed down quickly, leaving the area through another doorway.

"My Caliph, there are still workers outside the small room. Are they not in danger from the viruses?"

"Not at all, my friend. That room is completely insulated and is checked every morning for any possible leaks. The viruses will now be administered at my command by scientists in another room. Everything is operated by computer, of course. The men tell me that death will occur in no more than twenty seconds, and I'm curious to see how closely that timing will be in today's test. I am pleased that the agony and pain of these women will be brief. As you know, the Holy Quran demands that we respect women." Bakr waved his right arm and seated himself.

The two men watched the women carefully. The embraced each other as they sat on cushions. Suddenly, their heads jerked back. The blond tried to stand, her mouth wide open. A white foam erupted from her throat and quickly covered her naked chest. Bakr and Ali could tell she was screaming, but no sound escaped the room. The other woman simply slumped over on the cushions and never moved. Both their faces turned black. It was over.

Bakr applauded as he glanced at his watch. "Only fifteen seconds, Ali. A very successful test. I will relay my compliments to the team working on this project. As they leave their work tonight, they will be given access to some women who are new arrivals, as a reward for their efforts. Of course, their experiments will continue with larger groups of women to see if there is any reduction in the efficiency of the viruses. They will also test the germs in simulated weather conditions.

"One of this team's greatest challenges has been removing the bodies of animals and now humans who have been infected and died from the viruses. These germs are so potent that even a slight touch of the dead bodies can also bring death to the careless person. Here again, we owe a debt of gratitude to the old Nazi scientists who left their notes and diaries of their research. These saved us a great deal of time. If they had considered viruses instead of poison gas during the Second World War, who knows how that may have affected the outcome."

Bakr laughed loudly, and his friend joined in.

24

I N WHAT THEY THOUGHT WAS a show of solidarity to the nation, the two major political parties met in the same hotel, but ten floors apart, to choose their presidential candidates.

Jimmy Brickell's party discussion lasted only three hours and chose Senate Majority Leader Tom Falkner as their candidate. Falkner had finished second in the last regular presidential election. He was well known, had substantial voter approval, and would do well in the limited time for campaigning. The party was quite confident the presidential prize would be theirs.

Bob Stanford's party took most of an entire day to discuss and argue about candidates because there was no obvious choice. When they heard of Falkner's choice by the other party, they decided they had little chance in the election and chose an obscure governor from Wisconsin as their candidate.

Stanford and Brickell met in the hotel bar after their meetings.

"What a bunch of shit, Jimmy. This damn thing is a mess."

Brickell grinned at his friend. "With Tom Falkner as our guy, we're looking on the bright side."

Stanford downed his drink and ordered another. "I have to admit, you got the best of us there, but who knows how this will finally work out? Jimmy, if you don't mind sharing, what did your people think about the length of time before the election. And what about other candidates?"

"Good questions, Bob, and we spent a lot of time on them. Falkner has a lot of friends in the House and is going to talk to the Speaker about introducing a bill that will extend the campaign time before the election. He's going to ask for sixty days but will settle for forty-five. He'll get the bill through the Senate in short order. There's not a hell of a lot anyone can do if someone else runs for president—someone like Lucy Jennings, for instance. Can you believe that woman lobbied our committee to death to become our candidate? We're sure she'll run herself. But, as we both know, the parties can't control who runs, and neither can Congress or the Supreme Court, although they'll probably try."

"We agree. We'll support your effort on extending the campaign time. And just to cover our asses, we're going to file an emergency brief with the Supreme Court on the campaign time extension thing, even though our lawyers say it's really out of their hands. We're also going to ask the court to restrict the number of candidates, another long shot I think, but we're just covering our legal butts."

"Interesting," Brickell said. "The way this court has acted the past fifteen years, anything is possible. You and I both know that they've actually been making the law and not interpreting it. We really can't lose by filing the suits, but our lawyers agree with yours that they have no control over who runs."

"Let's hope they're right. Say, have you heard anything about Rose Akron and what she may do? I mean, she could announce her own candidacy if she wanted to."

"She could. But we haven't heard anything along those lines. What we do hear is that she's fed up with the job and fed up with Washington. So, I think she'll sit this one out and go peacefully back to Minnesota when it's all over."

"You're probably right, Jimmy. Whatever happens, it's going to be an interesting election."

25

ACTING PRESIDENT ROSE AKRON SAT speechless in the Situation Room of the White House. She had just listened to Israeli Prime Minister Ehud Shamir explain the findings of his agents within ISIS and the probable next move for that Islamic terrorist organization. With her was Vice President Carson Dansby, General Clint Courier, other members of the Joint Chiefs, and the president's national security adviser. They all stared at the screens of their videoconference with the Israelis.

Finally, she looked at Courier. "General, do you concur with the facts as presented by the prime minister and his analysis of the situation?"

"I'm afraid I do, Madam President. The facts echo many of our own findings, although I have to say that the Israelis have found hard, concrete evidence from their imbedded agents that we have not been able to duplicate. I think these facts are actionable and that we must move forward militarily immediately."

Akron nodded and turned to her vice president. "Carson, what are your thoughts?"

"I agree with General Courier, Madam President. I'm shocked that ISIS is this far along with weapons research and preparation. I don't think we have any choice but to strike them with every weapon at our disposal."

"Anyone else?" Akron glanced at all the others in the room. No one replied.

She turned to the screen and Ehud Shamir.

"Mr. Prime Minister, I want to thank you for your information and for contacting us so promptly. What do you propose?"

"I think we have little choice, Madam President. As General Courier and your vice president have stated, I believe we must attack ISIS now—right now—and destroy them and their weapons."

Shamir's staff nodded in agreement.

"If I may, Prime Minister?" It was Moshe Rabin.

"We are not certain where these weapons facilities are located. This morning we learned that two of our primary agents were discovered and executed. We know they were in Syria, but they were not able to identify the exact coordinates of their positions. This is a problem we are trying to resolve. ISIS has become adept at often moving their whereabouts when we least expect it. We believe we know general locations, but there is no way we can get specifics before we must take action. Under these circumstances, it may be necessary to use extremely heavy explosives, perhaps even nuclear weapons, over a wide area to make certain we destroy their main base and facilities."

"I agree with General Rabin," Courier said. "The time to move is now and with our most advanced weaponry. I emphatically endorse the use of nuclear weapons. The threat is that serious. Fortunately, the Joint Chiefs have scheduled training exercises so that our forces can attack immediately when I give the—"

"General, I believe I am still commander in chief, and I will give that order when I feel it is necessary." Akron was obviously annoyed. "The use of nuclear weapons is just as dangerous for us as it is for ISIS. I can't believe they would risk their own annihilation by using nukes against Western nations and the rest of the civilized world. They must know there is no going back once they are employed. I'd like you to present our latest satellite imagery to everyone here on both sides before a final decision is made." Akron's voice was firm and in control.

"But, Madam President, we have no idea when ISIS will use their weapons, only that they are very close to that time. And the whole point about what the Israelis have told us is that ISIS does not care how many people die from a nuclear blast as long as some of them survive. Waiting even a short time may—"

"Thank you for your advice, General. I'll look forward to seeing your satellite information. Mr. Prime Minister, do you have anything further?"

"Just one thing, Madam President. As I'm sure you know, we have been developing a new highly explosive bomb. Based on the bunker bomb technology you shared with us, this new weapon is many times more powerful than yours. It will penetrate many layers of concrete and steel. It may be useful in the near future. In the meantime, we will place our own forces on high alert. Let us schedule another meeting as soon as possible."

"I agree Mr. Prime Minister. I'll let you know when we have more facts before us. And I want to contact the British and French and let them know the situation."

"Of course, Madam President. I would caution that the more we involve other people, even our allies, the more chance we have of informing the enemy."

"I understand, Mr. Prime Minister. Thank you again for your help and support. I'll be speaking to you soon."

The screen went blank. Again, there was not a sound in the room.

Finally Akron spoke. "I'm adjourning this meeting until we have gathered more information. I'll ask the vice president and General Courier to remain. The rest of you are dismissed."

Akron waited until the other men had left and then turned to Courier. "General, I'm becoming more and more concerned, not only about your negative attitude toward me and my decisions recently, but also about your specific reaction to the information from the Israelis and your argumentative manner with me in front of everyone in this room. When I asked you to remain in my administration as chairman of the Joint Chiefs, I also told you that I expected there would be times when we disagreed and that I would respect your views as long as they were privately expressed, one-on-one, with me. You have broken that agreement. If you can no longer support me, I will expect your resignation today, as soon as possible."

Vice President Dansby was shocked. He had known General Courier for many years and shared the respect so many of his colleagues continually expressed for the man. At the same time, he, too, felt the general's remarks could have been better presented privately, between himself and the president. But considering what they had heard this morning, Dansby felt this was no time to make a change in the leadership of the Joint Chiefs.

General Courier stood up from his chair and came to attention. "Madam *Acting* President"—it was the first time he had ever used the term *acting* when he addressed Akron—"I understand completely what you are saying. You will have my resignation as chairman on your desk this afternoon. For the record, I will state once more that you and I took the exact same oath when we were sworn in to our respective offices—to preserve, protect, and defend the Constitution of the United States. While I respect you personally and the office to which you have been *appointed* by the Congress, I cannot respect your decision to wait for what I believe is an inevitable attack on this country and our allies by ISIS forces that could come at any moment. At this critical stage in our history, I intend to do everything in my power to uphold my oath and protect and defend my country." He saluted smartly, did not wait for a return salute, turned, and left the room.

Akron took a deep breath and turned to her vice president. "So what do you think, Carson?"

"I understand why you did it, Madam President. Courier was out of line. More than that. You are, after all, commander in chief. Still, I wish there had been some other way. I think we're going to need men like Courier in the weeks ahead."

Akron cleared her throat. "That's certainly true. I'd like your advice on replacements for Courier. I think his vice chairman may be too close to him to give me honest answers when the time comes."

"I'll get right on it, Madam President. I think you know I'm loyal, and I'll help in every way I can."

26

"TODAY, ALI, YOU WILL SEE how we instruct our new arrivals in Sharia law."

Bakr had just pressed the button for the second level of his underground headquarters. "You will see the remaining levels soon too."

"Every day is a revelation to me in your caliphate, my leader," Ali said. "What comprises the other levels?"

"The third level is a fully equipped hospital, Ali. We have the latest medical equipment and technology. Our doctors are among the very best in the world. As with many of our soldiers, these doctors have come to us of their own minds and hearts. And their skills give our men even more confidence when they face the enemy. There is so much to see, and the other levels will be equally stunning, I promise."

As the two men left the elevator, Ali was struck by the differences in what he saw now as compared to his previous visits to the other levels. Here, there were long corridors of well-lit classrooms. Each one was filled with men in military uniforms. Two or three older individuals stood at the head of the class, indicating they were leaders or teachers. Because of their clerical attire, Ali knew that they were imams or holy men, presumably of different ranks.

Bakr chose a class apparently at random. As he and Ali entered the room, the class came to attention. The two men walked to the front of the room and embraced the imams in the Muslim manner, extending their arms to each other's necks, and then took seats that had been made ready for them.

The senior imam turned to the class and spoke. "This morning, we are blessed and honored to receive our leader and commander, Abu Bakr and his friend Abdul Anwar Ali. This visit demonstrates our commander's dedication to the Holy Quran and to Sharia law. You have all been reading from copies of these two holy scripts and memorizing important sections. Today, I will call on you to demonstrate your faith and belief in the teaching of our holiest books. We will begin by simply moving from person to person in each aisle.

"As you have been taught, Sharia law comes directly from the Holy Quran and the teachings of the blessed Prophet Muhammad. It cannot be altered or changed in any way. Only an imam, such as I, can interpret it properly. Sharia law is not like other legal codes in any part of the world. Unlike the laws drawn up by the Americans and other Western infidels, Sharia cannot be interpreted by common men who claim to have studied their law and often speak in error. Sharia is the strictest law in the world and, because it is perfect, cannot be challenged or ignored. I realize that some of you, at first reading, may have found Sharia to be harsh and uncompromising. I promise you that you will learn to love Sharia as you feel its protective strength. Sharia is more than a discipline and statement of beliefs. It is a way of life.

"Because we have many subjects to cover, we will only discuss a few of the major principles of Sharia this morning. As I call on each of you, you will state five of these principles, loudly and with firmness, as a sign of your faith."

The imam gestured at the first man, who quickly came to attention. "Sharia law states that theft is punishable by amputation of the right hand. Criticizing or denying any part of the Holy Quran is punishable by death. Criticizing or denying Muhammad is a prophet is punishable by death. Criticizing or denying Allah, the god of Islam, is punishable by death. Any Muslim who becomes a non-Muslim shall be punished by death." The man saluted and took his seat.

The next man stood quickly. "Sharia law states that a non-Muslim who leads a Muslim away from Islam shall be punished by death. A non-Muslim man who marries a Muslim woman shall be punished by death. A man can marry an infant girl and consummate the marriage when she is nine years old. A girl's clitoris should be cut, according to Muhammad. A woman can have only one husband, but a man can have up to four wives. Muhammad, peace be upon him, could have more." Again, the man saluted and sat down.

Bakr was pleased and nodded as each man spoke.

The next man stood and saluted. "Sharia law states that a man can unilaterally divorce his wife, but a woman needs her husband's consent to divorce. A man can beat his wife for insubordination. Testimonies of four male witnesses are required to prove rape against a woman. A woman who has been raped cannot testify in court against her rapist. A woman's testimony in court, allowed only in property cases, carries half the weight of a man's."

"Excellent, my students," said the imam. "You give me great joy. And the final man?"

"Sharia law states that a female heir inherits half of what a male heir inherits. A woman cannot drive a car, as female driving leads to disorder. A woman cannot speak alone to a man who is not her husband or relative. Meat to be eaten must come from animals that have been sacrificed to Allah. Muslims should lie to non-Muslims to advance Islam."

As the last man seated himself, Bakr stood and applauded. "Would that the entire world lived by the words of Sharia you have repeated today," he said. "And my promise to you, my faithful followers, is that soon, through your efforts and sacrifices, Sharia law *will* become the only law of the world, God willing."

The entire group of men stood and cheered as Bakr and Ali returned their salutes and left the room.

"I thank Allah for allowing me to see this group of men this morning, Bakr. My faith is stronger now than it has ever been."

"Mine is renewed as well, Ali. I attend one of these classes every week. From now on, you will join me. It is a blessed experience."

"And what else do these men learn in this classroom level."

"As I may have mentioned before, my friend, we teach Arabic to those who do not already know our language. This is a first step and allows us to then instruct them in all other classes. Islam is next, again primarily taught to those who come from other religions. They must learn and love the Holy Quran and pray it daily. We have found that even those who claim to be familiar with and devoted to Islam must also take courses. Their past education may not be strong enough to meet our standards. Allah demands no less than perfection."

"This is all very wise, Caliph. I wish I had done these things with my own army."

The two men reached a corridor with two branches and Bakr led his friend to the left. "There are many other classes in this area, Ali, but we will next visit our combat training instruction."

"Ah, I know I will enjoy this, my Caliph. Combat training is my special love."

At the end of the corridor, Bakr and Ali came upon a room where soldiers were engaged in hand-to-hand fighting, led by a very large, scar-faced man with a patch over one eye, who was instructing. They entered, and the class immediately came to attention. There were heavy mats on the walls and floors. Above the wall mats, ISIS mottos were also displayed, along with a tattered and bloodied American flag pierced by a dagger.

Bakr returned the salutes of the soldiers. "Please do not allow us to interrupt. I see your instructor is my friend and comrade Saif Al-Hamsi. Saif and I have fought many battles together, eh, Saif?"

"Many, my Caliph. You have saved my life many times."

Bakr laughed. "Not as many times as you have saved mine, Saif." He turned toward the class. "This man is the very best example of an ISIS soldier. He would give his life for our cause and for each of you, and he has proven this many times in battle. Listen to him and watch him carefully. Everything he says and does can save your life. Now, please continue."

The men broke into groups of two and began to engage each other. Some used thick sticks; others, small knives. They also practiced a form of jujitsu Ali had never seen before. Al-Hamsi yelled encouragement and occasionally dealt a blow to one of the men.

Bakr noticed Ali staring at the men. "I see you are intrigued with our martial arts training, Ali. The method you are seeing comes from

Brazil and is taught in a separate class by Brazilian masters. They are the best in the world."

"Your men possess great skills that will serve them well in combat. And the knives I see them using seem to be real, Caliph," Ali said. "They do not practice with simulated weapons?"

"This is an advanced class, Ali, so real weapons are used. If men are wounded or killed, we believe that Allah has chosen another path for them outside of active combat."

Ali nodded and watched the men carefully. "They are in excellent condition, Caliph."

"They have never been defeated in close, personal combat, Ali. We have found that Western soldiers lose their bravery when they lose their weapons. Not so with these men. They need no weapons other than their bodies. My soldiers are feared throughout the Middle East for their willingness to sacrifice themselves to achieve victory."

"That is understandable, Caliph. I am most impressed."

"Now, perhaps you will also be impressed with this next area of our second level. Tell me, Ali, do you like films?"

"Films, my Caliph?"

"Yes, where the decadent Americans spend most of their time—watching films in theaters or on television."

"I do not care for such things, Caliph. I like reality."

Bakr laughed as they walked and directed Ali to a room with a stagelike setting. Bright lights, microphones, and cameras were scattered throughout the area, along with realistic background settings of all types. A Western-looking man was giving instructions to young men who were repeating speeches about the joys of ISIS as they were being filmed.

"This is where we make our own cinema, Ali. I am told these films are quite popular on American and Western television news. We also record our executions, which thousands of news programs show to millions of people. We film interviews with the hundreds of young people from all over the world who arrive here each day. They gladly tell other nations why they are attracted to ISIS and how they will devote their lives to our success.

"These productions are our best recruiting tool, Ali. They are part of what the Americans call 'social media,' and we have embraced this new tool and perfected its use. Even I have become quite skilled in manipulating these techniques to our advantage. Let us return now, Ali. I have some battle plans to show you and wish to explain the strategies we use. I am also anxious to receive your own suggestions for our improvement."

27

ARNIE MASON SAT SILENTLY IN the Supreme Court's informal meeting room, surrounded by his eight fellow justices. He had called the meeting to discuss the several issues Lucy had mentioned to him that were either already before the court or soon would be. He stared transfixed at his cell phone and the picture of Lucy Jennings taken in his bedroom the night before. She had become his obsession.

"Arnie? *Arnie!*" It was a very irritated Justice Carlos Stansby. The six men and two women seated around the table had many other things on their calendars and wanted to move forward with whatever was on the chief's mind. Mason had said this was an emergency meeting, but none of the justices knew what that meant. He was simply not himself lately.

"Ah, yes," Mason said, turning off his cell phone. "Sorry. That was an important message." He cleared his throat and consulted his notes. It was difficult for him to concentrate on anything except that image of Lucy Jennings.

"Ah, as you know, following our two national parties' recent selection of candidates for the interim presidential election, the court has received emergency petitions to expand the election date set by the Congress and to allow additional candidates to run for the office of president. I'd like to hear your general thoughts on both matters and your suggestions for preparing briefs on those subjects."

The other justices looked puzzled as they glanced around the room at each other.

Justice Sara Lipman, holding the so-called Jewish seat on the court, spoke first. "Arnie, you may not have heard of or read your latest reports, but there are two additional emergency petitions that have arrived. One suggests the new Twenty-Eighth Amendment is unconstitutional. The other—and this has all of us most curious—asks if the current vice president … You all know Carson Dansby, of course. The petition asks us to determine Dansby's status when and if Acting President Akron is no longer president."

Mason's face was bright red. It should have been *him* who called this new information to the attention of the other justices. It was one of his primary duties and a protocol that was never violated. "Ah, yes, Sara. I was about to get into those situations, and I apologize for my tardiness. I've had a lot of things on my mind lately. My apologies. Who would like to begin?"

"Chief Justice, with your permission, I'd like to read some research I've done on these issues and passed around to everyone. They've been in your box for a couple of weeks." It was Klein Wigginton, the newest and youngest member of the court.

Mason could do nothing but agree. "Of course, Klein. Please proceed."

Wigginton continued. "As you all know, there is nothing in the Constitution that speaks to either political parties or to the number of candidates who may run for any office. Both parties have submitted briefs asking that we disallow any further candidates in the election. In our informal discussions recently, I think the general feeling is that neither the Congress nor the Supreme Court can legally prevent anyone from running for president. We can, of course, just refuse to consider any of the briefs."

There were nods of general agreement among the justices.

"The easiest issue, we think, is the question of the unconstitutionality of the Twenty-Eighth Amendment. It appears to every member here that it is constitutional. My notes have various quotes, references, and precedents for your review."

Mason had regained some of his composure. "That's excellent work, Klein, and I appreciate you bringing all of us up to date. If there—"

"One last thing, Mr. Chief Justice, if I may?"

"Of course. Please continue."

"On the question of the status of the vice president when and if Acting President Akron leaves office, there is some disagreement among members of the court, and the preliminary discussions have been most interesting. First of all, the vice president was nominated by the acting president and confirmed by both Houses of the Congress. This is the procedure outlined in the Twenty-Fifth Amendment."

"Yes, yes. So what is the issue?" Arnie wanted to adjourn this meeting as quickly as possible and get back to his very personal business.

"Well, sir, the petition to the court raises several issues. The first is whether or not the vice president is actually an acting vice President, since he was nominated by an acting president."

"What?"

"Sir, I said—"

"I heard you, Klein. What the hell kind of nonsense is this? There's no such thing as an acting vice president in the Constitution or in any amendment. Is there?" Mason had begun to question his own knowledge of this new area of constitutional law.

"Here's the problem, Mr. Chief Justice. The petition asks what would occur if the acting president left office before the interim election. Would the vice president become president? Or acting president? Or is he technically an acting vice president and perhaps not even eligible to become president? And the really interesting question to me is this. If he does become president, what is the status of the person who was just elected to replace the acting president? Carson Dansby would conceivably be president, not acting president.

"The new Twenty-Eighth Amendment speaks only to replacing an acting president. Would that mean the election was invalid?"

"Ladies and gentlemen." It was Harley Cobbins, the oldest in age as well as service of all the justices. In his early eighties, Cobbins was from rural Tennessee and a graduate of Vanderbilt College of Law. His bushy eyebrows, wrinkled seersucker suits, and pink bow ties instantly identified him wherever he traveled. A staunch conservative, Cobbins had a mind that was still as sharp and clever as when he was a young law student. He was perhaps best known for being stubbornly politically incorrect and for having the foulest mouth in Washington. He was universally loved by all law students and lectured often throughout the United States. "Permit me to throw another turd into this cesspool of legal bullshit."

Several justices laughed loudly. Mason was not among them. He felt as though he was losing control over his court.

"I've been around this table and this Court for a long time. Some suggest I heard arguments in the first Supreme Court case, West v. Barnes in 1791. Actually, I was appointed a few years later."

There was more polite laughter.

"The point is that I've heard a lot of crap on a lot of issues, most of them nothing but nonsense. I think this is one of those. It's a dandy moot court argument in some fancy law school for smelly, unshaven law students, male and female, to debate. But it has no substance. President Akron, or Acting President Akron if you prefer, nominated Carson Dansby to be vice president, not acting vice president, and he was confirmed in an almost unanimous vote by the Congress, in accordance with the Twenty-Fifth Amendment. One of the few times the goddamned Congress has agreed on anything. That's all there is to it. The rest is bullshit. Besides, I haven't heard that Akron is going anywhere. So all this speculation is a waste of time."

"With respect, Justice Cobbins, I agree with everything you've said with the possible exception of the situation where Vice President Dansby would become president upon the departure of Acting President Akron." It was Wigginton again.

"Is Dansby then the president or acting president?" Wigginton continued. "And, if he is president, does that make the election to replace the acting president null and void? The petition asks us to address that issue, and it seems to me we ought to do just that."

The justices—except for Cobbins, who refused to participate—began to argue the point with one another.

Finally, the chief Justice rapped his knuckles on the table. "Ladies and gentlemen. Please. Let's come to order. I think Justice Wigginton has brought up some interesting questions. It seems to me that most of the points in that petition, as Justice Cobbins suggested, have, well, no substance. And the final point would have none if the acting president remains in office.

"Nevertheless, I think it's worth composing a preliminary brief on the subject, and I'll ask Justice Wigginton to prepare and distribute it to each of you as soon as possible. There is no need for us to take immediate action on the acting president issue as long as Rose Akron remains in office. The question of extending the election date belongs to the Congress, not to the Supreme Court. I would remind you that we are charged with interpreting laws, not writing them."

"Well, that would be a hell of a change from what we've been doing the last twenty-five years," Justice Cobbins announced loudly. "Oh, by the way, my secretary informs me that the Congress has just extended the period for presidential campaigning to forty-five days. Probably about forty days more than we really need. In any case, their action makes all of this a moot question."

Not wanting to get into another pointless discussion, and glancing at his watch to see if he was late for his meeting with Lucy Jennings, Arnie Mason adjourned the meeting.

28

"THIS HOSPITAL ON OUR THIRD level is what the West refers to as state of the art, Ali. As I've mentioned to you before, it has the very best equipment and doctors from throughout the world, who are pleased to serve our cause."

Ali's eyes widened as he walked through the hospital level of the ISIS underground headquarters. Even in the state hospital of his former capital of Damascus, there had been nothing like this. Nor was there in any Middle Eastern country.

"This area is one I want you to see, Ali. It is here our doctors can replace virtually any important organ in the body. We have found that bringing one of our soldiers back to full strength so that he can fight again saves ISIS time and money in training new bodies. It is also very good for morale."

Ali nodded. "And how do you locate these organs, Caliph?"

"We take them from captured slaves when the blood and body parts are compatible. Of course, we must be certain that we do not take unclean blood from Jewish slaves and other infidels and transfuse it into our soldiers. And if slaves are not suitable, we use organs from our own wounded soldiers who will not survive. Or, if they do survive, but can no longer fight, we take what we need from them because these men will no longer be useful to ISIS on the battlefield."

"And these wounded soldiers agree?"

"Of course. They know this will bring them to their heavenly rewards all the sooner."

"I recall in my own army, Caliph, that finding fresh blood supplies was always a problem, and we lost many men when blood was not available."

"You will be pleased to hear this, Ali. Many times our doctors can use new artificial blood they have developed when the correct natural blood cannot be located. They have found a way to inject oxygen into this artificial blood, and over time, it becomes part of the natural blood in the body. The Americans are still experimenting, trying to match this development. Once again, Allah has blessed us."

"Another remarkable achievement, Commander."

"But not the last one, Ali. Come down this corridor with me."

The two men walked up to a guarded entrance, received salutes, and entered a closely restricted area.

"Here we have joined mechanical and robotic science and medicine, Ali. When replacement body parts cannot be found or do not restore full combat capability to our soldiers, our laboratories have perfected artificial limbs especially designed to allow these men to use almost all of our weapons in combat. After they are attached to their bodies, our men go through a short period of retraining with a wide range of weaponry. Think of how much time and money this has saved us, Ali. And we developed a soldier who often cannot be wounded again in the same body area because it has been restored with a surgical, metal replacement. I tell you that a time will come, Ali, when we will develop an army, perhaps entirely artificial, that truly cannot be stopped."

"Amazing, Caliph. Just amazing."

"And now, if you have seen enough, let us return to my quarters."

29

LUCY JENNINGS WAS ON THE phone with Tom Falkner. She was mildly upset that he had been chosen by the party to be their presidential candidate, but she knew that things were far from finished. She also knew she could work on Falkner from several different angles, sex being the main one. Their last sexual encounter had impressed him, as it would with any man. Or woman, for that matter.

"Just wanted to congratulate you on your selection by the party, Tom. Can I call you Mr. President yet?"

They both laughed.

"Sorry the committee went the other way, Lucy. I know you wanted the top slot."

"That's not a problem for me, Tom. I'd like to discuss how I could switch positions to vice president on your ticket. That would certainly show strong solidarity to the voters. And my California constituency is bound to be a big help in the election too. How about talking over strategies about this change while you and I get together—say tonight?" Lucy knew this would get his attention.

Falkner thought briefly about telling Jennings he had decided to name Dante Caruso as his running mate. But why close that door right now? Why not give the situation a little more time? He recalled their wild sexual weekend of a few weeks ago. He'd like some more of that; in fact, he wanted a lot more. After all, some private—very private— discussions with Jennings might prove interesting in several ways. And perhaps he could pacify her with the offer of a high-level position in his administration.

"Lucy, that's a great idea. Let's get together soon. We have a lot to talk over. Tonight sounds good. There won't be much time for campaigning, as you know. Congress has given us forty-five days, and that's not a lot. I'll start on Monday. Of course, I want to make certain we're using your—eh—talents in the right places."

"You're always one step ahead of me, Tom," she said, not meaning a word of it. She had never met anyone who could outthink or outmaneuver her, in bed or out. "Tonight is fine. Your place or mine?"

"You know where my home is," he said. "Why don't you come over about seven? We'll have a few drinks, some dinner, and see what happens."

Jennings knew exactly what the horny bastard had in mind, and that was fine with her. She was growing tired of Arnie Mason and his pathetic devotion, and it was time for a change. Falkner was certainly more aggressive in bed. This meeting would be for all the marbles and give her a firm idea about how she could outscheme Falkner to get the top spot on the ticket. She was certain that an hour or two in bed with her would more than loosen him up. "That sounds great, Tom. Can I bring anything?"

"All I need is you, sweetheart," he said. Might as well let her know what he really wanted. "See you then."

30

ABU BAKR WAS DELIGHTED WITH the lovely redhead and admired her body as she stretched out on the silk sheets in his bedroom in the ISIS underground headquarters. The woman—a young American girl—had been with him all night and into the morning. Neither one of them had gotten much sleep. She was insatiable and matched Bakr's mood perfectly. He preferred American women because they were so gullible and willing to please. This one chewed gum constantly, which he did not care for. But today was very special. He had never felt this sure of himself and his mission, and it was all about to take place.

"My dear, I have a very pleasant job for you. I want you to go into the room next to this one and awaken my friend Abdul Anwar Ali, the Soul of the Sword. Perhaps you have heard of him?"

"I'm not sure, honey," she said. "Is he from Cleveland?"

"No, but it is not important. He is a very powerful and important man, and I have good news for him. I want you to awaken him the way you did to me throughout last night. It was most enjoyable, and you were exceptionally gratifying. Ali will please you, and when you are finished, please tell him I would like to see him as soon as he is ready. I can promise you he will reward you handsomely."

"Sure, honey," she said, slipping out of his bed. "You say the room next to this one? His name is Abdul or something?"

"Call him Ali. He prefers that. And you do not have to clothe yourself as you leave here."

She smiled at Bakr. "I wasn't planning on it, honey. By the way, your friend will have to go some to match you. You were great all night." She kissed him and left the room.

Almost two hours later, Ali entered Bakr's quarters, smiling broadly. "Caliph, you are too good to me. That woman you sent to wake me was most entertaining. I had to ask her to stop so that I could come to meet you. I hope I did not take too long."

"Not at all, my brother. I expected that you would take even longer. She is very difficult to leave and equally difficult to stop once she has begun her personal duties."

They embraced warmly and sat beside each other.

"Ali, this is a momentous day, and I wanted to share it with you. We are ready to send our biological teams out to their preplanned locations with the viruses. As I have said, this is the first step in our plan to weaken and then destroy all infidels—first the release of the viruses and then the detonation of our atomic devices. Our teams are awaiting my arrival and I would like you to be with me. And please wear your golden sword, my friend. There will come a time for you to display it."

Bakr stood and embraced Ali again. He waited for him to adjust his sword and then took him by the arm and left the room. He led him in a different direction on this same level than Ali had gone before, with no need for the elevator. In a few minutes, they entered a large auditorium filled with about two hundred men, who rose together and began to cheer as they saw Bakr.

The caliph, still holding Ali's arm, stepped up on a central stage, gestured for his friend to be seated next to him, and approached a microphone. The crowd became silent as he spoke. "The blessings of the prophet be upon you and your families," he said. "This is a great day for our caliphate. You have all been chosen most carefully for your intelligence and dedication to our cause. Yours will be the first step in our cleansing of this world of infidels and your entry into heaven."

Applause and cheering interrupted Bakr.

"You have spent many hours training and receiving your instructions. When you leave here this morning, you will return to your leaders, who will have final orders for you and give you everything you need to accomplish your divine task.

"Before you leave, I wanted you to meet my beloved friend, whom you have seen with me for the past few weeks." Bakr gestured to Ali to accompany him at the microphone. "This is Abdul Anwar Ali, the president for life of Syria. But he is better known throughout the Middle East and feared around the world as the Soul of the Sword." Bakr stepped back and pointed to Ali, who drew his sword and waved it over his head. The crowd stood once again and cheered.

"As you reach your destinations, I want you to know that I will be fighting and praying for you. And if it is Allah's will that I join him before our task is complete, it is Ali who will lead you." He raised Ali's arm with his and shouted, "Al-ḥamdu lillāh" (Praise be to God)! The cheers were deafening.

Back in Bakr's private quarters, the two men were greeted by three beautiful, naked Arabic women, who led them to private baths. There they spent the afternoon enjoying the women and refreshing themselves with food and drink.

"My Caliph, I must tell you that I was brought to tears of joy by your remarks this morning," Ali said. "Never have I felt the power of your words and the dedication of your men more than I did with you today. I am your obedient servant, and I swear by Allah to give my life to complete your plan and bring about the end of times as told to us in the Holy Quran." Ali bowed his head to Bakr.

"I know you will do so, my brother, and, God willing, we will both live to see the fruits of our labor and a new Islamic world of power, peace, and love."

"Caliph, I have one question about the men we saw this morning. I saw soldiers of many different races and, I assume, from many different countries. How have you made it possible to train them all?"

"Truly, this has been accomplished only through the guidance of Allah, bless his holy name. The men were chosen from the specific countries they will now return to with their weapons or they have been trained in the language and customs of the country where they'll be sent, spending time there whenever possible. Their appearance was most important for obvious reasons. They will dress and act quite naturally in accordance with the practices of the countries they are being sent to.

Those men who have an obvious Middle Eastern appearance will be sent only to countries that already have large Middle Eastern populations. As you know, we have been infiltrating many countries with our people for years, slowly building significant strength. Now our men will blend in wherever they are sent, trained and skilled in the normal behavior of their respective countries."

Ali nodded. "So, from that group this morning, the Americans will go to the United States, the French-speaking men will go to France—"

"Exactly, my friend. Fifty different countries and cities will welcome what they believe to be their own citizens. There are four men to a cell in each location. Their passports and other identity papers are perfect. They will have plenty of money, and safe houses have been prepared for them in advance. They have memorized their plans and have alternate procedures in place. In addition, we have previously sent men to all our target locations to assist these cells when they arrive."

Ali continued to be amazed by this man and the depth of his planning and resolve. "Forgive me, Caliph, for asking. I know we cannot—will not—fail. But if a few of your cells are discovered and prevented in some way from completing their assignments, then—"

"There are two teams for each location, Ali. The first teams will be sent out with their viruses to fifty different cities today. If they cannot complete their assignment, the second team will follow them. In fact, we will send the second team even if the first teams are successful. It is Allah's wish that we accomplish this task, and we will not fail Him."

"And what of these atomic weapons, Caliph? When my own people were studying these possibilities in the last war, we could not get past the problem of discovery by the enemy. The size and radiation from the devices would give us away."

"Ah, but no longer, my friend. Many things have stayed the same in our world, but science and technology are not among them. The ability to create powerful, lightweight, portable atomic devices that will fit in a backpack and to shield those devices have been made possible due to new technology. And the proof that Allah, blessed be his holy name, is helping us, is that the materials we use were discovered by American and Chinese scientists who have been working with us for the past year.

"The Chinese, in particular, have invented a complex radiation shield that cannot be detected. In fact, this shielding is also used here at our underground headquarters to protect us and our laboratory work. Of course, all of our atomic devices are sheathed in this material as well. Our major problem, as it is with the viruses, is getting safely into the countries and cities to distribute and detonate our weapons. We have worked on resolving that situation and have great confidence we will succeed. And our two-team strategy will apply to the nuclear devices as well. I know you will be pleased to hear that, even if our nuclear teams are discovered, they have been instructed to instantly detonate their devices wherever they may be."

"And what will they use for the detonation?"

Bakr nodded and stood up. "Both the viruses and nuclear weapons will be set up and detonated using cell phones by the men in the units I have just described. As you are aware, our brothers throughout the Middle East have used these phones most effectively against the Western soldiers. Some of our weapons will also be swiftly delivered by our ... air force!"

"Air force? But, Caliph, you told me you did not have aircraft or missiles."

"And so I did, Ali. Now, let me show you another surprise. Come."

Bakr took his friend by the arm and walked to yet another part of his headquarters. This time, they again made use of the elevator, which took them down to the fourth level. As they exited, Bakr guided Ali through a series of doors that he had not seen before, leading into yet another laboratory. Here he saw what appeared to be a long, concrete-paved roadway with distance measurements annotated on each side.

"Ali, behold my air force!" Bakr clapped his hands, and several men in white suits immediately appeared.

Bakr spoke to the men in Arabic. They bowed and disappeared into an adjacent room. Suddenly, Bakr pointed to the tall ceiling above them. Ali gasped as he saw a half dozen small, silent flying objects appear and head toward the two men. They looked like mechanical birds and could not have been more than two feet long.

"My Caliph, they are approaching. Should we—"

"Have no fear, Ali."

The devices passed over the heads of the two men and released square packages, which fell harmlessly at their feet.

"So what do you think of my air force, Ali?"

"But what are these flying things, my Caliph? I have never seen their like."

"Again, science has taken giant leaps, my friend. I know you saw the large American drones during the last war. In fact, it is rumored that one of them launched the missile that destroyed your palace. These are miniature drones—small but most powerful. As you can see, they weigh just over two pounds and are slightly longer than two feet and about the same in width. They are strong enough to carry the lightweight virus capsules and atomic devices for at least a thousand feet at a low level and are virtually undetectable." Bakr was obviously proud of these weapons.

"And your scientists invented these … these aircraft?"

"No, we did not invent them, Ali. The Americans and Chinese were the inventors; our people just perfected them. They are easy to assemble and fly swiftly to their targets. We will use these drones because some of our objectives are so well-protected or isolated that our manned cells cannot place the canisters and atomic packs close enough to assure destruction. In that case, our men have been instructed to use drones to detonate them as closely as possible to the target.

"Let us consider the American White House, for instance. It is well guarded, as is their war building, the Pentagon. In this case, we will send our drones, which will fly undetected to these and other buildings and detonate their weapons up against or close to the targets. In fact, drones have already been flown onto the grounds of the White House and Pentagon several times by their own citizens who hate their government. They were not detected until after they had landed."

Ali was dumbfounded. "But how will you get these aircraft—these drones—from here to the target countries?"

"They are already there, Ali! They have already been distributed to our agents in the fifty locations over several months. You saw how small and light they were. We simply disassemble them here and send them by well-concealed methods to our men in the selected cities. These men have detailed target information and will load and prepare the drones at the proper time.

"At the appointed hour, they will take positions close to the objectives, carefully conceal themselves, and then reassemble the drones and fly them to the chosen target. Because of their unique configuration, the drones can be assembled in a matter of a few minutes. We have had some problems with the new lithium-ion batteries that power the drones. They are so potent they occasionally burst into flame. Our scientists have been working without stop to resolve that issue. But nothing must keep us from our strict schedule of attack. We are committed to a certain date and time, and we will hold to that even if our equipment is not perfect. The Americans and their allies know nothing of our drones, Ali. It is a foolproof plan, God willing."

Ali shook his head and bowed to Bakr. "Truly, you are blessed by Allah, Caliph."

"You are kind, my friend. But enough of these demonstrations. Let us return to those lovely women and see how responsive they may be."

31

FALKNER AND JENNINGS WERE STILL locked together on the floor of his living room, clothes scattered all around them. They had both put off discussing political plans for the time being. Lucy wanted a good physical workout after spending weeks with that fragile Arnie Mason, and she knew that's exactly what Falkner had in mind too.

Falkner had a fine selection of top-shelf, single malt scotch, and after dinner, the two of them had lost track of how many drinks they had before getting down to what they both wanted the most—each other. Little time was wasted on small talk. They had managed to discuss the forty-five-day campaign time period just set by the Congress and to speculate about who else might run for the office.

Then Lucy had taken charge, as usual. She knew what Falkner liked, and he was easily excited. Men were such fools, she thought, and so much alike. They all wanted the same things—breasts and butts—and once they got them, they were lost and completely in her power. And her breasts were the best money could buy—$10,000 per side and worth every penny. No one had ever been able to tell they weren't all natural, and she laughed to herself as she watched Falkner.

When he was finished, Lucy expertly feigned the guttural sounds and cries he expected.

They stopped long enough to refresh their drinks and head for his bedroom. Falkner was ready for a long, sweaty night and suggested they take a shower together. That was just what Lucy wanted. His shower was huge and had two long benches with soft, waterproof cushions ready-made for their activity.

Jennings had enough sexual tricks in her repertoire to put on a show, and shower sex was one of the best of her specialties. She had perfected her skills over many years, with both men and women. Women were so much better at sex than men, she thought. They took their time and knew instinctively what would continually arouse and please their partners.

Falkner was no challenge for her at all. In a few minutes, he lost complete control, uttering what could only be described as rabid animal sounds. She had to steady him to keep him from falling as he sank to his knees in the shower.

"Maybe we should take a break," he moaned. That was when she knew she had him.

"Sure, baby. You've worn me out anyway," she said. "Let's get back into bed and just cuddle and talk things over." *Cuddle my ass*, she thought. *I have you where I want you, and I'm going to get everything I've been planning.*

As Falkner lay beside her, she reached alongside the bed for her purse and withdrew a single sheet of paper and a pen. The wording was exactly the same as the pledge Falkner had drawn up for her just a few weeks ago. It stated simply that, at the appropriate time, he would announce Jennings as his vice president. It had the present date and a place for his signature.

"Tom, I thought turnabout would be only fair play. You asked me to sign this exact same pledge when I thought I might be the presidential nominee of the party, choosing you as my running mate. Now you can do the same for me. I promise I'll show you how grateful I can be." She handed him the paper.

Falkner was exhausted, but he wasn't stupid. Lucy Jennings was the best sex partner he had ever had, and he'd had quite a few. But there was no way he was going to make the bitch vice president. She'd probably poison him the next day and be quick to put her hand on the Bible when they swore her in as president. But he didn't want to lose that incredible body completely. He'd sign the paper now and figure out a way to tell her later that the party wanted Dante Caruso for VP, and he couldn't talk them out of it. Then he'd give her some minor post, something to suit her particular talents. Maybe secretary of sexual development!

He nodded at her. "Sure, honey. Fair is fair. Give me that pen." He signed his name with a flourish. "There you go."

"Thanks, Tom. You won't regret this. Now let me know when you're ready for more."

32

THE GOVERNORS OF THE STATES of Iowa and New Hampshire were closeted with Speaker of the House Caruso and Senate Majority Leader Falkner. The governors were fighting mad.

Iowa spoke first. "I don't need to tell anyone in this room that, since 1968, the state of Iowa has had the first and most prestigious presidential caucus in this nation. America looks to Iowa to identify its selection for president. There is simply no way we can have a presidential election without the Iowa caucus."

New Hampshire was ready for this. "Tom, the fact is that no one can understand what the hell Iowa does in a caucus. Dammit, we don't even understand what a caucus is. Why, you have a bunch of old, white farmers meeting in someone's bathroom to say they favor some candidate. What in God's name does favor mean? Your, uh, system—if you can call it that—doesn't make any sense. Here's what I mean. The way you handle things, people who want to vote for someone but can't get enough of their neighbors to agree with that choice have to give up their candidate and pick someone else. And if they have a tie vote in that bathroom, they flip a coin to choose a winner. Probably do the same thing to see who pees first too. That's ridiculous."

"Now, just a minute Ben," said Iowa. "In the first place, it's not a bathroom, it's a kitchen. We usually meet in a kitchen or a dining room. We've only met in a bathroom once, and that was some time ago. I think it was when that senator from New York was running. And you call us old, white farmers? Why that's all you have in New Hampshire.

And you only have one and a half million people in your puny state. We're twice as big as you are and twice as important because we're first and always will be."

Both governors were red faced.

Senator Falkner, already the choice of his party for the presidential election, rapped his knuckles on the table, smiling at one and all.

"Governors, please. The simple fact is that there isn't enough time to hold a caucus or a primary in any state. And the Constitution doesn't require one or even mention it. This is one time when a state being first, or second, doesn't amount to a hill of beans. We have forty-five days to elect a president—even less now—who will move that woman out of the White House, and we'll use that time the best way we know how. That doesn't include a caucus or a primary in any state." Falkner was openly pleased that the torturous process for selecting a president was being bypassed this time. When he was president, he would see to it that a national primary was put in place.

New Hampshire was mad as hell. "Look, Tom, the Constitution guarantees us certain rights and liberties and this is one of them. I won't—"

"On the contrary, Governor." It was House Speaker Dante Caruso. "The Constitution doesn't say a thing about elections or caucuses or primaries. Those things were left up to the states to decide. The only thing the Congress does is set a date for the election, and we've done that. It's about a month from now, so the argument for a caucus or a primary is really over. Sorry, but that's where we are."

"We'll sue," Iowa shouted. "We'll sue the Congress and the Supreme Court and both of you. I'll be goddamned if we'll have an election in this country without Iowa folks being first."

"And we'll join that suit in New Hampshire. We'll get the Supreme Court to shut this whole damn thing down. Why, we don't even have to have an election. We have a president or acting president, so what's the hurry?"

It was Falkner again. "The hurry, as you put it, Governor, is that forty-five states, yours among them, passed the Twenty-Eighth Amendment to the Constitution. That makes it a law. We have to have an election to get rid of this so-called acting president, and there's no way around that. The Supreme Court has already ruled that the Twenty-Eighth Amendment was legally processed and approved by the voters and that's that."

The governors began whispering to each other.

Finally, New Hampshire spoke. "Gentlemen, maybe you've heard of my state's motto. 'Live free or die.'" Well, since we can't live free and have our own primary, we have plenty of folks in New Hampshire who are ready to die for the right. And I'll be the first one to lay my life on the line."

Falkner and Caruso could hardly keep from laughing.

"And let me add to that," said Iowa. "Our state motto is, 'Our liberties we prize and our rights we will maintain.' Nobody messes with our liberty, and you people in Washington have gone too far this time." He slammed his fist on the table and stood up.

Not to be outdone, the New Hampshire governor shouted out, "That goes double for me," and slammed his fist twice on the table. Then both men left the room.

Falkner and Caruso sat silently and looked at each other. Then they both started laughing.

"You know, that wasn't half as bad as I expected," Falkner said.

"Actually, I enjoyed it," Caruso said.

"I propose a toast," Falkner said, opening a bottle of water.

Caruso did the same.

Falkner raised his water and shouted, "Live free or caucus!"

Both men continued to laugh.

"Dante, tomorrow I announce that you are my choice for vice president, and we start campaigning. Now let's go get a real drink."

33

LUCY JENNINGS WAS SO MAD she couldn't speak. She sat on the edge of Arnie Mason's bed, both hands tightly clenched.

"That son of a bitch," she finally said. "I have a signed statement from that bastard Falkner promising me the vice presidency. He can't do this to me. And what can this Cuban refugee from Florida do for him that I can't do? Not a damn thing. Well, he won't get away with it."

"Arnie, listen up." She stood beside the bed, glaring at him, her arms on her hips. "I want you to call another private meeting of the other justices as soon as possible. No. Do it tomorrow. Early. I want you to tell them to vote against that suit Falkner's people filed preventing anyone else from running for president. I'm going to announce my own candidacy as soon as you meet with those old bastards."

"But, Lucy. I can't tell them how to vote. You know that. We've talked about this before. There's no law that keeps anyone from running for president."

"Arnie, we need to be certain about this. If you expect our relationship to continue, you goddamn better well tell your buddies down there to do whatever it takes. I don't care what the procedure is called. You know how to do it. You've told me a dozen times how you all sit around that conference room before a big case and bullshit about it before you decide on an issue. Well, this isn't even a case. It's just a request for an emergency opinion or whatever the hell you call it."

"Lucy, there's no such thing. The Supreme Court just can't hear frivolous requests for opinions. That's not how it works. There are strict procedures for cases to come before the—"

Jennings waved her hands over her head. "Don't give me that crap, Arnie. I don't care about your procedures. I just want this stopped. And now. Figure out a way."

"Lucy, the simplest way is for the court to refuse to hear the request from Falkner because it's frivolous. Then it just disappears."

"Then make it disappear, Arnie. Or I'll disappear. And you'll never see me again."

Mason knew she meant it.

34

AZIM HASAN WAS NINETEEN YEARS old. He had been captured in an ISIS raid in Iraq when he was only thirteen. His captors were quick to notice how intelligent the boy was and how quickly he adapted to ISIS training and beliefs. Azim's father had been killed earlier in the war; in order to survive, his mother had become a whore for the soldiers. His new life within ISIS was far better than he had ever known before, and he rose in leadership and combat skills even at his young age. He was selected for intensive language training in French and showed a great aptitude. After two years, his knowledge and accent were perfect. At eighteen, he was chosen to spend a year in Paris, practicing what he had learned and getting a feel for the people and country. France had always had a large Muslim population, and Hasan blended right in with them. There were thirty men in his class, all of them quite proficient. To fail in this group, or in any assignment, meant instant death, of course.

He and his three ISIS cell members were seated on the floor of their tiny apartment in Paris. The city had been chosen as the first European capital to receive the viruses because of past successful attacks by ISIS in France. During the three weeks they had lived there, the men carefully located the sites for the devices previously selected by their trainers. The Eiffel Tower would have been a perfect spot because of its height, but ISIS realized there was too great a police presence involved. Personally placing weapons there was out of the question. And using drones in locations like that, with little concealment, was just not practical.

Before the team had left the ISIS camp, their trainers and commanders had planned not only the targeting but also the specific dates, times, and backup plans for their attack. They would position their devices in four major locations throughout the Paris Metro stations, as well as in the four tallest commercial buildings around Charles de Gaulle Airport. Their final spots would be the largest military base closest to Paris and inside French government headquarters in the Hotel Matignon. Military bases, subways, and central government locations would be a common theme for all the ISIS targets.

They practiced for a full week with walk-throughs at all the chosen sites. There were plenty of police officers and military personnel everywhere, but the four young men with backpacks looked like typical Middle Eastern college students, and they attracted no attention. Even if they had, they all spoke French fluently, and their identity papers were perfect. As they approached the chosen time for releasing the viruses, the men prayed, checked their equipment again, and left the apartment one at a time, a half hour apart, heading in different directions.

Over the next two hours, they arrived at their target locations and were able to place the devices without interference. Drones would not be used yet for these targets. All virus canisters would be triggered by cell phones at the moment determined by their ISIS commanders, to coincide with the most crowded time of day.

The four men returned to their apartment when they had completed the placement of their virus weapons. They prayed once more and then dialed the numbers of their devices at the same moment, destroying their cell phones afterward in the fireplace of their apartment. After shaking hands and embracing, they sat and waited. It was no accident that their apartment was less than a block from a major Metro station. They knew they would be among the first to feel the effects of the viruses. After that, Paradise awaited them, God willing.

35

THE NATIONAL NEWS NETWORK (NNN) was nervous. The well-respected network had agreed to show one televised presidential debate, but no one seemed that interested. All the other networks had refused. After all, the country was on the brink of war, and the United States already had a president. All this business about a new constitutional amendment that required an interim presidential election to remove Acting President Rose Akron was confusing to most people and very difficult to explain. Editorials all over the country pointed out that she had done nothing wrong, so why should she be replaced? Others argued that she had done nothing right, either—in fact had accomplished nothing at all—and that was the reason she had to go. Overall, the situation had served to boost the favorable ratings for Akron, who had her hands full to say the least.

The chief anchor for NNN, Karl Strong (real name Conrad Schwartz) had been complaining about being designated to moderate the debate since it had been scheduled. He had just had his hair whitened to show up better on television. But his real complaint was that he truly disliked the three candidates. He thought Senate Majority Leader Tom Falkner was an arrogant asshole. Falkner felt he should have been president a long time ago and kept referring to his strong second-place finish in the previous regular election. He had been nicknamed "the Crown Prince" and "President in Waiting" by the *New York Times*, and it had stuck in the minds of the people.

Wisconsin Governor Todd Hamling was an extremely overweight person who didn't seem to realize he was running for the highest office in the land. He had left the state of Wisconsin exactly once in his life to visit an uncle in Ohio. Hamling's nickname in his home state was "Ham Hock." He persistently complimented Falkner and on one occasion had even said he thought Falkner would make a great president. Not much conflict there—nothing to draw viewers and ratings.

And then there was former House Speaker Lucy Jennings. What more could be said about her and her personal history without being sued? It was common knowledge in Washington that she was sexually promiscuous, to put it nicely. As a matter of fact, Karl Strong had once propositioned Jennings, causing her to break into fits of laughter. He had also heard that the only reason she was running was to get even with Falkner for not naming her as his vice president.

The white-haired anchor sighed as he looked in the mirror to check his makeup. The network had better double his salary after this one. Glancing at his watch, he saw there was only ten minutes before airtime. He sighed again and stood up to walk out onto the stage and check the lighting. If the candidates were already on stage, he could exchange phony pleasantries with them.

Lucy Jennings was testing her microphone as he approached. Governor Hamling was staring at Jennings with his mouth open and completely ignored the anchor's outstretched hand. Well, Strong had stared at her many times himself, so he couldn't blame the poor Wisconsin hick.

"Lucy, how are you," Strong said. "Good to see you again. You're looking lovely."

Jennings looked up and grimaced at the man. She placed all men in two categories. The first included those she'd sleep with to get what she wanted, and that was a pretty large group. The other included those she wouldn't sleep with no matter what she could get for it, and the NNN anchor was in that much smaller category. He was simply loathsome, and she let him know it. "Oh, hello, Karl. Had your hair whitened lately?"

"Now, now, Lucy. Let's not get off on the wrong foot. By the way, are those breasts real?"

"That's one thing you'll never find out, Whitey," she said.

Governor Hamling continued to gawk at Jennings and ignored Strong completely.

Well, the hell with all of them, Strong thought. He seated himself at his anchor desk, checked his notes, and let the NNN stage manager handle the rest. Tom Falkner waited until the last minute to make his entrance, as usual. He was truly acting like a president in waiting. Strong decided he would enjoy the expected fireworks between Falkner and Jennings and at least have some fun with this so-called debate.

The audience in the auditorium at Florida State included only a few hundred people in it, most of them students who appeared to be quite high on something. In any case, they were acting and sounding ridiculous. One fraternity group held up a sign that said "Hey, Lucy. Are they real?" Strong winced at that and hoped this wouldn't be a total disaster.

After brief introductions and a quick explanation of the Twenty-Eighth Amendment requiring this interim election, Strong got down to cases. He had a long list of tough questions. But as he had known would happen, none of the candidates answered what they had been asked. Falkner and Jennings were pompous asses, and Hamling couldn't seem to take his gaze away from Jennings. No one wanted to discuss the issues.

"Karl, I have a personal statement to make." It was Jennings.

Why not? Strong thought. The debate was going nowhere, and he had to fill the time with something.

"Yes, Speaker Jennings. We'll give you and the other candidates the same opportunity for some personal remarks."

Jennings showed her approval and took a deep breath. That caused Governor Hamling, breathing heavily, to audibly groan and look like he would cry.

"Karl, first I want to remind the millions of Americans watching tonight that as speaker of the house, I was honored to have my name placed in a House bill as the *first* candidate to be chosen as acting president. Unfortunately, the Senate adjourned before taking action. Tom Falkner was behind that, Karl, and now I want to show you and the American people why I've been saying that Senator Falkner should not be president." She withdrew a file from her briefcase and walked over to Karl.

"I have already given a copy to your people in the control room so that they can show it on television as you and I read it. This is a signed statement from Senator Falkner promising to name me as his vice presidential candidate before the campaign began. Obviously, that didn't happen. I believe this proves he is a liar and deceiver and can't be trusted to hold the highest office in the land." Jennings returned to her podium.

Strong didn't know what to say, so he ad-libbed. "Senator, do you have a reply?"

Falkner continued to smile at the camera. "Not really, Karl. The lovely former Speaker, who was defeated for reelection in her own district by the way, apparently can't take a joke. She begged me to sign that statement as a—a keepsake, I guess you could call it. We had been seeing each other socially, and when I broke off the relationship, she wanted something to remember me by."

Jennings was outraged. "Remember you by? You jackass. I have plenty to remember. Most of it is you falling asleep instead of paying attention to me. You are an arrogant fool, and no one in his or her right mind would vote for you. And no—*no one*—has ever broken up with me."

"Now, now, Lucy," Falkner replied. "You do look beautiful when you're angry."

Jennings turned bright red and walked off the stage. Governor Hamling followed close behind her, wiping his sweating brow, his mouth still wide open. It was the fastest anyone had ever seen him move.

After thirty-five years on the air, twenty of them as chief anchor, Strong was speechless. He stared at Falkner, now all alone on the stage, who continued to smile at the camera. There were seventeen minutes remaining in the debate, and the network had not prepared for this kind of scenario.

After stuttering for a moment or two, Karl managed to say, "We now return you to our studios."

36

"THERE'S NO QUESTION THAT THIS is a biological attack in France by ISIS, Madam President. That's been confirmed. The French have found capsules or containers with ISIS markings. They don't know exactly what this germ is, but their best guess is poison gas or some kind of virus."

"What's the death toll now, Sherm?"

"Just over ten thousand in Paris and its suburbs; that includes some military personnel at a base outside Versailles. This may be just the start. They don't know how to combat it. French officials are sending air and blood samples to our CDC in Atlanta for analysis. By the way, many members of the French government have been infected and have died. A virus or bomb detonated close to their main ministry building. Death occurred very quickly."

"Good Lord. Ten thousand. It doesn't seem possible."

A brief knock sounded on the staff door to the president's office, and her executive secretary entered hurriedly. "Sorry for the interruption, Madam President, but there's a call from the British prime minister."

"Thanks, Janice." Akron turned to her phone bank and pressed a button to an encrypted line.

"Darren, I'm sure you're calling about what's happened in Paris."

British Prime Minister Darren Graves sounded frantic. "Actually, Madam President, I'm calling about our own situation. We've been hit by the same kind of attack. It's biologic as it was in Paris, but we have no clue what it is or how to stop it. Our people are discussing vaccinations and antidotes, but we have nothing to go on, and nothing we've tried has worked so far. One of the devices went off outside Westminster, and I'm afraid to say our government is in real jeopardy. This is definitely an ISIS attack. Even our largest military base and our tubes have been hit. You should do everything you can to prepare for and combat this plague, or whatever it is. Sorry, but I have to go now."

"Thank you, Darren. I'm calling our Centers for Disease Control right after this. I'll contact you if we come up with anything." They both hung up.

"Sherm, use the usual channels to get our civil defense on full alert and schedule an address for the nation with all networks within the next hour."

Boyle was already on his feet, heading for the door. "I'm on it, Madam President. And boss, the Secret Service wants to move you and the vice president to separate secure locations as soon as possible."

"Already? I suppose that's the smart thing to do, but I hate to give in to those ISIS bastards. Okay, tell them I'm ready any time."

Alone in her office, Rose Akron put her head in her hands. There wasn't time to cry, and she didn't even feel like crying. She was mad as hell. Was this all her fault? If she had reacted faster to the warnings from the Israelis, could this attack have been prevented? Was it too late now?

She had to prepare for an address to the nation, but first things first. She called the interim chairman of the Joint Chiefs and told him to put the armed forces on full alert. She knew the chiefs had already prepared a comprehensive plan of attack against ISIS in all of its known and suspected locations throughout the Middle East, and she ordered the chairman to put that into effect. Then she called her speechwriters to prepare remarks for her address. Finally, she made some personal notes of her own.

37

"**G**OOD AFTERNOON, MY FELLOW AMERICANS. By now you have heard the horrid news from our friends in France, Great Britain, and Germany about the attacks by ISIS on the people, government, and military of those countries. Japan and China have also just been attacked. The weapon appears to be some kind of virus and is quite potent. The death tolls are mounting. We are providing all the assistance we possibly can.

"I want you to know, first of all, that we have not yet been attacked. I do not want to alarm you unnecessarily, but I would not be doing my duty if I didn't tell you that we expect ISIS to try something in this country before too long. I'll be asking our Centers for Disease Control in Atlanta to work nonstop on an antidote or vaccination for this virus, and I'm confident that they will make swift progress.

"Just an hour ago, I ordered our armed forces to attack ISIS positions on a continuing basis throughout the Middle East. Because we are not certain of the exact position of all ISIS locations, one of the main elements of this attack will be carpet bombing by our B-52 fleet and other bombers in the area of Syria, where we believe ISIS may have its main bases. We are also striking in major portions of northern Iraq, Libya, northern Iran, sections of Saudi Arabia and Egypt, and Yemen and Lebanon, despite having been denied permission for access by several of those countries.

"I want to be clear that our attacks will include participation by American ground forces, as well as elements of the army, navy, marines, and Special Forces. I realize that I pledged to you that I would never send our own ground forces to the Middle East, but I hope you can appreciate that we are now at war, and the circumstances have changed drastically. Many of our allies are also participating, even though their militaries are suffering from the viral attacks. In addition, we are being joined by armed forces from Japan and China, the first time in recent history that these two countries have fought on the same side. This has obviously become a world war by any definition.

"As I was walking out to this microphone, I was handed a message from Russian President Dimitri Obloff telling me that Moscow has just been struck in the same manner as in the other countries I've mentioned. The primary targets in all countries appear to be metro or subway systems, along with government buildings and military bases.

"Our leading experts in biological weapons offer this as their best advice to you. If you live close to any of the three target locations I've just mentioned, stay in your homes. Keep your doors and windows closed. If you have an air-conditioning or heating system, turn it off. The safest place in your home may be a basement if you have one. Otherwise, keep your family in a room or other safe place without windows. Some communities with supplies of breathing devices such as gas masks are distributing them to their people. Unfortunately, these materials are quite limited. Therefore, I have ordered civil defense units throughout the United States to make this breathing equipment available in their areas on a first come basis. Biologists tell us that a good rainstorm can clear the air and may be the best natural weapon against the virus until we find a chemical defense or develop a vaccine.

"I am declaring a nationwide state of emergency while we prepare for this ISIS attack. I have sworn to protect and defend this nation, and I will do everything in my power to do so. Stay close to your radios and televisions for further updates and listen to your local civil defense agencies. I hope that many of you will join me in praying for all nations. God bless you all and God bless the United States of America."

38

CAMILLE OKO HAD BEEN A chief biologist at the Centers for Disease Control for eleven years and had just reached her thirty-second birthday. She was not married. Her area of expertise was the analysis of viruses and the preparation of vaccinations against their spread. Oko was of Japanese descent and had chosen her work because of the stories that were repeated to her as a child about her grandparents, who were burned to death by the atomic bomb dropped on Hiroshima during World War II. She had been told there was no cure for radiation poisoning and, at an early age, had decided that she would dedicate her life's work to developing cures for complex diseases that had plagued the human race for centuries.

Just slightly over five feet tall, Oko had olive skin with a smooth and delicate texture. Dark, almond-shaped eyes completed her lovely features. She had an excellent sense of humor and laughed often with her lab assistants.

When her office phone rang, she was surprised to hear who was speaking to her. It was Acting President Rose Akron in Washington.

"Good morning, Ms. Oko. This is Rose Akron."

"Good morning, Madam President. I hope you are well. And please call me Camille."

"Thank you. And my name is Rose. I've just spoken to Director Crosby at the CDC, and he gave me permission to speak to you personally. Of course, it's about the viral attacks around the world and which we anticipate will occur in our own country very soon.

The Israelis were fortunate to capture one of the cells that was about to release the viruses in the Tel Aviv area. For the first time, we have possession of four canisters of the virus. The Israelis are keeping two for their own testing, and we are flying two down to you for your analysis. They'll be arriving in an hour. The director says you have the best mind in this field, and we need your finest work on these samples."

"Madam President—Rose—of course my team and I will do everything in our power to identify the viral agents and, if possible, prepare a vaccination to combat them."

"I know you and your colleagues will do your best, Camille. I'm sure I don't have to stress that time is of the essence."

"I understand, Madam President. You can count on me and the entire CDC."

Oko hung up and said a silent prayer that her talents would be worthy of such a challenge.

39

ENERAL CLINTON COURIER HAD NO doubt he had made the right decision. ISIS attacks around the world were increasing. Over a hundred thousand were now confirmed dead. This weak American president had finally decided to attack, but it was too little, too late. Courier believed the only chance for his country to survive was for him to take charge. America was fortunate not to have been attacked so far, but Courier knew it was inevitable.

He and his friends commanding the Joint Chiefs had just met in secret to finalize their plans. When General Cort Simmons, who had initially expressed reservations about Courier's plan, finally agreed to join them, Courier knew they would be successful. While Courier had been asked to resign as Joint Chiefs chairman, he was allowed to keep his full rank and was serving his last few weeks before retirement at the Pentagon without any specific assignment. At two o'clock this afternoon, he and the Joint Chiefs would approach the bomb shelter beneath the White House and gain admittance to the war room where Acting President Rose Akron and her staff were located. The guards outside the well-protected facility had been chosen for their loyalty to Air Force General Chuck Clark. None of the Joint Chiefs loyal to Courier had been replaced—a major error on the part of this female president, who had again shown her ignorance of basic military procedures.

Courier carefully put on his freshly pressed marine dress uniform. While he usually allowed one of his aides to prepare and assist him, he was all alone in his austere Pentagon office. He had arranged his uniforms himself for many years and no longer needed one of the nicer trappings of his high four-star rank.

He would finish soon and then leave the Pentagon and join the Joint Chiefs in a secret location known only to them. They would proceed by emergency military vehicles to the White House and to the underground facility that housed the president. Once inside, he would inform the president that he was relieving her of her responsibilities and, along with the Joint Chiefs, was taking charge of all governmental functions during this wartime period. The other military officers on duty inside the war room had also been hand chosen by the Joint Chiefs and would immediately support the takeover.

Courier would inform the president—by then the *former* president—that even though she was under house arrest, she would be treated with the utmost courtesy and receive everything she required. The chiefs had prepared a residence for her in a safe house known only to them and some loyal staffers. When the crisis was over, Akron would be allowed to return safely to her home in Minnesota. Courier would work with the Congress to set a date for new elections. He had no desire to become a dictator.

He glanced again in the full-length mirror. His decorations fully covered the left side of his chest. He could name every one and describe the circumstances under which he had received each award. It was common knowledge that he was the most decorated soldier in the history of the United States.

Courier saved the most distinctive honor for last. He opened the safe in his office and removed the nondescript, leather-covered box. Carefully, he placed it on his desk and slowly opened it. This was his Medal of Honor, the highest military decoration awarded by the United States. It had been presented to him by former President Cory Fredericks, in the name of Congress. This designation caused many Americans to refer to the award erroneously as the Congressional Medal of Honor. Congress actually had named a different medal for themselves.

There were three versions—for the army, navy, and air force. As a marine, he wore the navy medal. While Courier, and every Medal of Honor recipient, was authorized to wear the decoration at all times, on a light blue, silk neck ribbon, he wore his only on special military occasions or when requested by the president. He felt that this occasion demanded that it be worn.

As he placed the blue ribbon around his neck, he remembered the citation read to him by the former president. He knew it word for word:

> Lieutenant Colonel Clinton C. Courier distinguished himself conspicuously by gallantry and intrepidity at the risk of his life above and beyond the call of duty in action with an armed enemy in the Wardak Valley in Eastern Afghanistan. While leading his marine combat team, Colonel Courier, along with his men, was ambushed by a well-armed enemy insurgent force. Coming under heavy fire, and with several of his men severely wounded, Colonel Courier first administered emergency medical aid to his fallen men. Then, without regard to ongoing, withering fire, he engaged the enemy, receiving several wounds that pierced his body armor. Colonel Courier, disregarding his own wounds, then recovered several of his wounded men, dragging them to safety at continuing risk to his own life. Courier engaged the attackers, killing six enemy combatants and injuring three more.
>
> Colonel Courier's unwavering courage, selflessness, and decisive leadership while under extreme enemy fire saved the lives of many members of his combat team. His extraordinary heroism and selflessness above and beyond the call of duty are in keeping with the highest traditions of military service and reflect great credit upon himself, his team, and the United States Marine Corp.

Courier rubbed his right arm over the scars from one of the wounds he had received that day and thought again of his men and the hellfire they had been through. He had made certain they'd all received high-level decorations for their bravery and perseverance. He checked himself once again in the mirror and then carefully positioned his military field grade cap with its gleaming visor on his head and left his office.

He stepped into the elevator and pressed the lobby button, pulling firmly down on his uniform purely out of habit. As he stepped out, several passing military personnel of all ranks saluted him. As a Medal of Honor recipient, even the president was required to salute Courier first. He acknowledged each of them by returning their salutes and watched one young airman come to attention with his mouth and eyes wide open.

Courier walked to the main exit of the Pentagon, showed his identification, saluted several more times, and stepped outside the building.

***

The small, silent drone released the ISIS virus capsule, and it detonated just as Courier glanced up at the sky. Thirty-seven personnel dropped dead instantly. Medal of Honor recipient, Marine General Clinton C. Courier, was one of them.

40

BAKR AND ALI HEARD THE bombing in the distance and felt the vibrations only faintly. They had seen the American president's speech. Bakr was not impressed.

"She can try whatever she wishes. There will be no defense to our attacks."

"Is it true, Caliph, that rain can wash away the virus?"

"To some degree, Ali. We did experiments in this area, but we do not know exactly how much rainfall would be required to dilute the virus and make it less effective. Our scientists have told me the three combined viruses are so powerful that they sometimes have a reaction against each other. They added a buffering agent to the viruses before our first teams departed. With Allah's help, this will continue to make them effective.

"This morning, I ordered our atomic unit cells to move up their departures even if their equipment is not totally cleared for action. Some of the American airborne attacks have made lucky hits on a few of our other bases. Still, the defensive structures around these underground headquarters can withstand even a direct hit. My main concern now is that some of our cells have been captured or have not carried out their missions because of equipment failure. I have ordered the second teams into action, but several of our bases are unresponsive."

Ali wished to calm his leader. "Caliph, you are still the beloved of Allah and receive his special protection. And we have heard many reports of our successful attacks."

"Yes, Ali. Some of the world's great powers have been driven to their knees. God is truly great, my friend, and I know we will prevail."

Ali nodded. "The Americans are still a potent force, my Caliph. It is my prayer that they will soon succumb to both of our weapons."

"As they surely must, Ali, God willing. One of our virus teams was located and captured by the hated Israelis. Our agents tell us that those Zionist pigs are working frantically on protection against the virus. I am certain they will have no success. In any case, the atomic cells should be detonating their weapons in that country and others very soon."

The bombing sounded like it was closer but still not cause for alarm.

"Come, Ali. Let us go to our bomb shelter. It is too soon for my death due to a fortunate strike by the American dogs."

41

COURY ATKINS AND DONALD BARTON were leaders of ISIS Atomic Team 5. Their target was Washington, DC, specifically the White House and the Capitol building, as well as the Pentagon.

Coury and Donald were native born Americans from Minneapolis, both twenty-two years old. They had gone through high school together and through one year of college. They had become radicalized as teenagers. Their neighborhood was predominately Muslims who claimed to be peaceful and loyal Americans. The imam of a local mosque, an ISIS agent for several years, had used the loveliest women in his holy place to entice the two young men, promising them their virginity in heaven when the boys gave their lives for Allah. They had soon sworn allegiance to ISIS in a private religious ceremony among their friends in the mosque.

At the same time, they kept their American friends and interests. To any casual outside observer, Coury and Donald appeared to be normal American boys, dating local girls and talking football and baseball. They both worked in a local hardware store and were careful never to draw attention to themselves. Their parents and non-Muslim friends were completely unaware of their conversion and dedication to ISIS.

They left America when they were nineteen, flew to Turkey, crossed the border into Syria, and then joined ISIS. All of this travel was paid for by their mosque in Minneapolis, which also established their advance contact with ISIS. They never informed their parents of where they were going and never contacted them once they had joined ISIS.

Over their three-year training period, the men studied the Holy Quran, learned fluent Arabic, and dedicated themselves to intense hand-to-hand combat training. After two years, they were told that they had been selected to detonate atomic weapons in Washington, their former nation's capital. Despite the realization that this would mean their instant death, Coury and Donald were overjoyed and thanked Allah throughout their daily prayers.

Because of the significance of their targets and the difficulty involved in placing their weapons in positions where they could do the most damage, the men were told to avoid capture by all means and to detonate the devices as close as possible to the targets. ISIS scientists felt the explosive force would still be strong enough at a distance to cause serious destruction.

42

INSIDE THE SECURE BOMB SHELTER beneath the White House, Acting President Rose Akron looked over the latest casualty reports from around the world. The deaths from the ISIS virus had now reached a half million. Large video screens displayed areas in the Middle East being bombed by American and other coalition forces. Akron had spoken to Camille Oko at the CDC only an hour ago. Oko had reported some promising results from her team's analysis of the contents of the capsules captured by the Israelis. The vaccine developed a few years ago to combat the Zika virus had had some positive effect on the ISIS germs. They were proceeding as fast as possible to find a cure and develop a vaccine. Oko informed the president that they had nicknamed the virus Armageddon X.

She was thankful that Washington, DC, had not received any ISIS attacks so far, but she had reports that viruses had been released in New York, Boston, Philadelphia, Saint Louis, and Los Angeles. Further attacks on other major cities were inevitable. Heavy rains were forecast in Washington and they might help, from what Akron had been told. Americans always seemed to band together in circumstances like these, and she knew they would again now as the crisis mounted. The air and land attacks against ISIS in the Middle East were underway on a full-time basis, and she hoped for positive reports soon.

"Madam President. I've just been informed that the Pentagon has been struck by the ISIS virus, delivered by small drones aimed at all entrances and air-conditioning systems." It was her chief of staff, Sherman Boyle.

"Drones? For God's sake, Sherm. What about casualties?"

Boyle was silent for a moment. "I'm trying to get an accurate count now. But there is one thing." He paused again, searching for the right words. "General Courier was exposed as he was leaving the Pentagon and died instantly."

Akron put her head in her hands, a position that was becoming all too common lately. Despite their recent confrontation and Courier's resignation, she admired and respected the man. It was no way for a soldier to die.

The secured subbasement of the White House suddenly shook as if struck by an earthquake. Akron guessed it was part of an ISIS attack but had no way of knowing it was the first atomic detonation in the capital. The war room they were in was completely sealed and presumed safe even from a direct hit. No one knew the bomb was a small-yield weapon detonated at some distance from the White House.

"Sherm, find out what you can about that."

Boyle was already on a secure phone and taking notes as fast as he was able.

In the distance, another explosion sounded. Everyone in the room looked up at the flickering television screens for information.

Suddenly, they all went dark.

"Madam President, telephone communication is limited. The shielding on our secure phones is helping a little. Our video should also return soon. I'm told we have had two atomic detonations. The first was just above us, close to the White House. The other was outside the Capitol building, which was also the target of a virus weapon some time ago. Fortunately, most of the Congress had also been moved to the shelters beneath the Capitol. Apparently, both bombs were delivered by drone. But their power sources—some kind of battery—either caught fire or exploded before they could be placed directly up against the White House and the Capitol. There was still severe damage. Emergency decontamination crews are at work now.

"Our military has been deployed as per our emergency procedures. Several of our bases around the country have received viral attacks but were already in a protective posture after hearing about attacks in other nations. There have been injuries and deaths, and I'm waiting for more information. That's the latest."

"Sherm, contact the vice president and bring him up to date. I have a feeling this is going to last a while. When you get hold of him, I'd like to speak to him."

43

CAMILLE OKO WATCHED THE VIRUS samples in her petri dish. Her team had worked nonstop for days on modifying the vaccine they had developed against the Zika virus, hoping their changes would create a slightly adapted version that could be used against the ISIS Armageddon X virus.

Oko stared intently at the transformed Zika virus in her dish. This was perhaps the fiftieth attempt they had made. She carefully removed a tiny sample and placed it inside a sealed biosafety console containing Armageddon. As she watched under a microscope, the two viruses combined and then mutated. There was only one way to tell if this was a good reaction and a possible vaccine—test it on her lab animals. The problem was that all of the modified Zika viruses up to this point had been just as deadly as Armageddon X. With every possible vaccine they had tried, most of the animals had died, some almost immediately, others over an hour or two, in extreme pain.

Oko never tired of trying new combinations. Through heavily protected arm and hand sheaths, she used a hypodermic to extract a small amount of the new modified virus and injected it into a lab mouse. Several assistants gathered around the compartment and watched. The mouse began to run in circles, stopped, sneezed, and continued to run around its small chamber. It began to drink thirstily from its water bottle, ran again, and then went over to the food dish and started to eat. The technicians looked at each other hopefully.

"Let us not get our hopes up too high," Oko told them.

They waited for an hour and then injected the mouse with Armageddon X. If Oko had been able to cross her fingers inside her protective gloves, she would have done so. Her assistant started a stopwatch as they both stared intently at the mouse. It showed no reaction at first, and then it seemed to squat down. Five seconds, ten. The mouse started to move. It turned in circles and then went directly to its water device and drank for some time. Fifteen seconds, twenty. More drinking, scratching. Back to the water. Thirty seconds. This was twice as long as any other mouse had survived.

"We must watch for at least an hour, Kim," Oko said to her assistant. "In the meantime, please inject a guinea pig and a spider monkey with the same modification. Wait and hour, and then inject them with Armageddon. Let us see how they react. If these tests are successful, we will inject a dog and cat. Perhaps we have something here."

Oko's team spent the night in a room down the hall from the laboratory. Her assistants took turns checking on all of the test animals. Other than showing extreme thirst for a time, they all survived and were eating and sleeping normally. Their behavior, appetite, and eyesight were good. Twenty-four hours later, there were still no apparent aftereffects.

"Martin is next," Oko said.

Martin was the name of one of the baboons used for experiments in the laboratory. Martin and others had been bred specifically for this purpose. Their use was still controversial but allowable under present law. The type of baboon they used most closely conformed to a human being in almost all respects. The team was glum. They had inevitably become very attached to Martin.

"I will give Martin the two injections myself," Oko said. "I know how you all feel. I feel the same. Think of it this way. Our country and many others around the world have been under attack for two days. Hundreds of thousands of people have been killed. All of our other animals have survived so far. If our test with Martin proves successful, we may have found the answer and be able to produce a vaccine that can save many lives."

Once again she filled a syringe with the possible vaccine and reached through protective gloves into Martin's cage. The animal came to her arms immediately, apparently thinking he would receive a good scratching. He and Camille Oko were longtime friends, and they trusted each other completely. Oko injected him quickly with the vaccine.

The agonizing wait began again. Oko scratched Martin's head and stomach. He opened his mouth and uttered a strange sound she had not heard before. He released himself from her arms and walked slowly around his enclosure. He picked up a toy and threw it at Oko, usually a sign that he wanted to play. Then he walked over to his water bottle and drank all the liquid very quickly and lay down. There was a loud sigh from the lab assistants who thought Martin might be dying. But he stood up very quickly and brought his water bottle to Oko, signifying that he wanted it filled. An hour later, he was still drinking.

An assistant had prepared the second injection—this one containing the Armageddon virus. And, after another hug and scratch, Oko injected Martin while someone started a stopwatch. Again, the seconds went by. After a full minute, Martin blinked several times and again walked over to his water bottle. He drank heavily and sat down and then threw another toy at Oko. She reached in and began to play with him. Her staff applauded.

"It would be good to celebrate, but this is a crisis of the most serious proportions," she said.

The standard procedure for the lab team would be to wait another twelve hours to see if the subject, Martin in this case, reacted negatively. Then CDC Director Shelton would call the president to get clearance to try the vaccine on a human subject. There were prisoners on death row who had agreed to try unproven vaccines and signed releases to that effect. Their families received a sizable payment for this service, or they designated the funds to a charity. This had been done only twice in US history, once on the devastating flu epidemic of three years ago and on the Ebola virus about twenty years ago when it turned into an epidemic and was spreading rapidly. While this was a last resort, Camille Oko felt the dire circumstances called for this action.

44

AKRON HAD HAD ENOUGH—ENOUGH OF everything. She had involved her country in yet another world war and American men and women were being killed throughout the Middle East, something she had promised would not occur during her administration. Now the White House, the Pentagon, and the Capitol had come under biological and nuclear attack. And the good man who had opposed her, General Clint Courier, was dead. She felt like a complete failure.

"Madam President, here's Vice President Dansby." Boyle handed her the phone.

"Carson, are you okay?"

"Fine, so far, Madam President. We're in such an inconspicuous location that I don't think we're a major target. And I'm told that this heavy rain that's started is about the best thing to clear or at last dissipate the virus."

"Yes, the CDC tells me the same thing. Do you need anything from me?"

"No. I don't think so. My staff has the same information you do, and Sherm filled me in on a few other points. Is there anything I can do?"

"Just stand by, Carson. If you have any suggestions about what else I can do, please pass them on."

"I can't think of anything right now." He paused. "Take care of yourself, Rose. The nation needs a firm hand now like it never has before."

"Thanks, Carson. I don't know if I have the right hands for the job, and I'm worried."

"We're all worried, Rose. Stay safe."

"You too."

As Akron hung up, she was interrupted by her secretary. "Madame President, it's Camille Oko at the CDC. She says it's urgent."

"I'll take it. Camille? It's Rose Akron. How are you doing?"

"Fine, Madam President. I have good news. We have developed a vaccine for Armageddon. It has been tested successfully for humans under emergency protocols, and we have begun to duplicate it here in Atlanta. We have also sent it to independent laboratories that are in safe areas around the country, as well as to our allies. We should be ready to begin to vaccinate in twenty-four hours."

"Camille, that's great news! And it's raining heavily here in Washington."

"In Atlanta as well, Madam President. And there is one more thing that is important. The ISIS virus is apparently a combination of three other viruses we have identified. While this composition is extremely potent, it is also extremely erratic. In fact, we have seen our samples from the Israelis undergo what I can only call a self-destruct stage. It appears that, over time, each virus attempts to gain superiority over the other two. In effect, they are trying to cancel each other out. The result is that they become much less potent. This enabled us to develop a safe vaccine."

"Camille, this has to be a good thing."

"We believe so, Madam President, but we are continuing to monitor the viruses. In the meantime, the virus that is still being released may continue to be extremely lethal, and vaccination is essential."

"When we have time, Camille, I want to hear all about your experiments and how they proved to be successful. You've done an incredible service for your country, and I thank you from the bottom of my heart."

"You are most welcome, Madam President."

"Camille, what's that noise? It sounds like some kind of animal?"

"Oh, that's my ape, Martin, Madam President. He wants me to rub his tummy. Martin is just one of the heroes of this whole situation. I'll tell you all about it soon."

Akron smiled for the first time in several days. "Give Martin my best, Camille, and thank you again."

Akron took a moment to reflect. At least she had presided over one catastrophic event successfully. A killer virus had finally been thwarted. But there had been over a million deaths around the world. And her country and others were facing atomic attacks, as well as biologic. But the victory over the virus was still a victory.

She had done the best she could, knowing full well that it was not enough. She was simply not prepared for any aspect of this job, but a world war with an attack on her country was far beyond her capabilities. It was time for a change—a stronger, take-charge personality. Delaying any longer could mean further disasters for her country.

"Sherm, get the secretary of state for me."

"Right away, Madam President." It took Boyle only a moment to locate the man, and he handed the phone back to Akron.

"Harold? This is Rose Akron."

"It's good to hear your voice, Madam President. How are you holding up?"

"Not too well, Harold. Are you safe?"

"I think so. I guess you know that two bombs have exploded close to the Capitol. Most of us were in this shelter in the subbasement. It's pretty old, and the military with us is concerned about leaks from radiation and the virus. I guess I was lucky to be visiting the House Speaker when this all got serious. I have to tell you that a lot of congressmen are unaccounted for. They could be safe; we just don't know."

"Good, I'm sending you a private message by fax and secure computer transmission to the Speaker's office. Be on the lookout for it."

"I will. And, Rose, keep the faith."

"I'll try, Harold. I'll try."

Akron turned to her chief of staff. "Sherm, I have a confidential message I want you to transmit to the secretary of state. You can reach him through the House Speaker's personal e-mail and emergency fax number." She handed him a single sheet of paper. "You may read it before you send it."

Boyle unfolded the sheet. The message was only one sentence long. It read:

The Honorable Harold Carter
Secretary of State
Dear Mr. Secretary:

I hereby resign the Presidency of the United States, effective at noon tomorrow.

Sincerely,
Rose K. Akron
Acting President

45

"SHE'S DONE *WHAT?*" ARNIE MASON shouted. "But, she can't—I mean, what—why?" The sound of thunder and heavy rain could be heard outside his apartment.

"Look at it from her point of view, Arnie." It was Justice Harley Cobbins on the phone. "She never wanted the job. Then the job got tough. Then they tried to maneuver her out of office with that bogus Twenty-Eighth Amendment. Then the whole world went to war. Our country is being attacked; she did what she could. She put the CDC on full-time development of a vaccine for that damned virus. The truth is that no one could have done more. We don't know what comes next. And now she wants out. I don't blame her a Goddamned bit."

"But ... but we're in the middle of a presidential election, for God's sake, Harley. It would have been over in a couple of weeks. What will this do? What about the election?"

Cobbins chuckled. "I think those three candidates are shit out of luck, Arnie. The fact is that we already have a president now. His name is Carson Dansby."

Mason was still upset and not thinking well. "But he can't do that. He's the vice president. And he was never elected, just appointed by that woman."

"And confirmed by the Congress, according to the letter of the Constitution, Article II, Section 1. He's for real, Arnie."

"Where? Where does it say—"

"Come on now, Mr. Chief Justice. You know history as well as I do. You know the routine. We've gone through this before. Nixon's VP, that crook Spiro Agnew, started all this. When he resigned, Nixon chose Gerry Ford for VP under the new Twenty-Fifth Amendment. Gerry was a damn good Speaker of the House, by the way. We wouldn't be in such a helluva mess if he was still around."

"Ford? But that was so long ago. What has this got to do with—"

"Then Nixon resigned. We wanted to impeach and convict him, but he was too fast for us. Tricky Dicky. So Ford moved up from VP and became president.

"Goddamn it, Harley, I don't need a history lesson from you. I just want to know—who the hell is president?"

"Like I said, that would be President Carson Dansby, the former vice president. And I think it would be a nice gesture if you swore him in yourself."

"But we have an election in progress to choose a new president. And the country is at war." Mason had visions of an enraged Lucy Jennings, who would dump him as soon as she heard the election was over.

"Well, if you could get your mind off of those fabulous tits you've been playing with and showed up at your office, you'd know we've already received an emergency petition from the governors of Iowa and New Hampshire asking that we declare the election null and void.

"By the way, Arnie, I've polled our brothers and sisters on the court, and there are eight votes in favor of the petition. It's all over, brother. Now all we have to worry about is a war. By the way, doesn't it make you wonder why those ISIS boys don't think enough of the Supreme Court to bomb our own building? What do they know that we don't?" He laughed and hung up.

Mason tried to calm down. He had work to do—serious work. He was told there had been no nuclear explosions close to his building and that the rains would limit any virus contamination. Still, he was supposed to remain in his apartment with the windows closed. All members of the court had shielded phones in their quarters, and he quickly called Justice Sara Lipman.

"Sara? It's Arnie. Yes, yes I know. It's terrible. Yes, she has really resigned. No, I don't know where she is. I assume in that bunker under the White House. Are you safe? Good. If you're up to it, I need you to do a special favor for me. I would appreciate it if you would swear in the vice president. Yes. It's a practical matter. I'm working on that emergency petition from those two governors. You can swear him in by videoconference. I know you have a setup at your home, and I'm sure he does too. We can swear him in in person later on. If you have any objection, I'll find someone else. You will? Oh, thank you, Sara.

"Now, one more thing. I'm going to call the court together by videoconference in just a little while. I'll wait until you have sworn in Carson Dansby. Since Rose Akron has resigned, and Dansby will be sworn in as president, that makes the interim election null and void. Harley Coggins just called and told me that eight of you had already met and agreed that we should issue a statement declaring the election void *ab initio*. We can formalize that by videoconference, if it's still working. Then let the media tell the nation. Is that okay with you? Fine, Sara. Thank you so much. Stay safe, and I hope to see you soon."

46

ARON ROVNER AND JOSEPH LIEB had joined ISIS two years ago. They were Jews who claimed they hated their Jewish upbringing and religion. They pledged to ISIS leaders that they would deny their former faith and study to become devoted Muslims and work on behalf of the coming caliphate.

They were also Jewish spies working for Mossad, the Israeli secret service.

During their two years with ISIS in Dabiq, Aaron and Joseph had trained with Muslim Arabs and had actually fought alongside them. They had been tested many times for their commitment, including their participation in the rape of Jewish women and the beheading of captured Jewish soldiers. Their job for Mossad was to infiltrate and learn as much as possible about ISIS, its plans, and its weapons. Primarily, they were charged with pinpointing the exact coordinates of the central ISIS headquarters.

Even after their demonstrations of loyalty, the two men were searched and interrogated often. They were never really trusted but were allowed to continue as ISIS laborers and, occasionally, as soldiers. They had no access to ISIS secret battle plans or details about weapons. Part of their Mossad training was in navigation and positioning using the sun, moon, and stars. But this would never do for the pinpoint coordinates needed for precision bombing. Mossad had devised a clever miniature GPS device. The two men had hidden the small tool in one of their body cavities just before they were first captured.

The ISIS guards believed that touching the deep private areas of a male Jew would bring contamination and death, so they searched the Jewish converts only in their clothing and outer bodies. Muslims apparently never saw the contradictory logic in their duplicitous beliefs—touching male Jews brought death; touching female Jews brought sexual satisfaction.

After being tortured and interrogated for several weeks, Aaron and Joseph were able to conceal the GPS device in a loose brick in their sleeping quarters. Over time, guards paid less attention to them, especially after they had fought against the Americans and allies on the battlefield.

Using the small but powerful GPS late at night, they were able to determine specific coordinates for the ISIS main headquarters in Dabiq. Knowing how important this information would be to Mossad, they worked for months to find a way to transmit or otherwise send their information to Tel Aviv. The possibility of being discovered was a constant, serious threat. So many other Jewish spies had been found out and murdered. The two men finally decided that escape was the most logical solution, despite the many risks.

They planned their method over several weeks. Their scheme was to travel south the 430 miles to their headquarters in Tel Aviv, along the coast of the Mediterranean Sea, and to move only by night, dressed as Muslims. They could speak Arabic fluently and quote competently from the Quran. Traveling a minimum of ten miles a day, they estimated they could reach Tel Aviv in no more than six weeks. They would carry no weapons and find food wherever possible along their journey. They both committed the coordinates of the secret ISIS base to memory and made a pact that, if they were captured and identified, they would break off and swallow the poison capsules concealed in false teeth in their mouths. Under no circumstances would they allow themselves to be tortured and reveal their real identities and special knowledge of Mossad.

Their initial escape was simple compared to what lay ahead. They had been part of a group of men who transported supplies for the hidden Dabiq camp through underground tunnels from several concealed locations in the desert. These groups were changed frequently, as were the tunnel locations, and the men were blindfolded so that no one would become too familiar with the specific sites. Nevertheless, over their two-year captivity, they'd finally gained enough knowledge about one tunnel to feel comfortable with using it to escape.

It was several miles to the seacoast, and they lost valuable time hiding from ISIS patrols and from Syrian villagers who supported ISIS and would have turned them in for rewards. Once they caught sight of the sea, they turned south toward Israel. Only the country of Lebanon separated them from their home, but it was controlled either by ISIS or Syrian troops or the occasional Special Forces patrols from several Western countries. The desert alongside the sea could be rocky and flat and made hiding difficult.

The men stole food at night from villages, if they were lucky. Most of the time, they were left to finding insects and small animals in the desert to live on. Here, their Mossad and ISIS training came in handy. Both organizations had required them to take instruction in desert survival.

Their knowledge of the night sky and occasional use of their small GPS was helpful for identifying their location as they traveled, but following the sea south to Israel was the simple system for getting back to their base. They ran into many dangers along the way, including occasional minefields, which they avoided only with great skill and luck.

But the worst development was when they were discovered by a Lebanese patrol one morning as they were sleeping. Most of the time, the two men would head inland for a mile or so to find better cover and then hide in the best place available. Just before dawn one evening they had chosen a cave in a cliff that had been used by others and was occasionally checked by soldiers. Two armed Lebanese guards awakened and beat them, not knowing who they were or what they were doing.

Aaron and Joseph, speaking fluent Arabic, pleaded ignorance and explained that their village had been attacked by forces they did not recognize, and their families had been killed. They told the soldiers they were trying to reach another village where they had relatives. They guards discussed this among themselves and decided to turn the two men in to the first ISIS patrols they could find, hoping for a reward. The guards had begun to tie up the two Jewish spies when Aaron, who was the better hand-to-hand fighter of the two, overcame one of them, killing him and taking his weapon. The other guard shot and seriously wounded Aaron, before he, too, was killed by Joseph, who buried both soldiers.

For the next week or so, Joseph tended to Aaron's wounds, trying his best to save his friend. But he had only a little food and water taken from the guards and no medicine. He struggled to move Aaron by night, as other men would come searching for the missing soldiers they had killed.

Despite Joseph's efforts, Aaron passed away. Joseph buried him as best he could, praying the traditional Jewish prayer for the dead, the Kaddish. "Have mercy upon him; pardon all his transgressions … Shelter his soul in the shadow of thy wings. Make known to him the path of life."

Checking his position, Joseph estimated he had just over a hundred miles left to reach Israel, perhaps ten more days of travel. He was excited and determined to reach his base and give Mossad his information. He kept to the plan he and Aaron had devised, traveling primarily at night and living off the land. He carried one of the weapons he had taken from the soldier he'd killed, but he knew that, if he were captured with it, he would be executed immediately. He compromised by hiding the gun when he was resting during the day.

Finally, Joseph saw an obvious border crossing in the distance. It was heavily guarded by both Lebanese and Israeli forces. It was just after noon, so he headed inland once again to find shelter for the night. He quickly disposed of the guard's rifle, realizing that he could be shot by either side before he'd even had time to explain his situation. He had no Mossad identification and knew that any man who turned himself in to the Israelis could claim he was Jewish and a spy just to try and survive. His appearance was terrible, his clothing torn and filthy, his hair and beard grown too long and disheveled. He decided to spend a day reconnoitering the general terrain to see if he could locate a way through the guarded border crossing.

It took him two days to find an area he believed he could crawl through at night. He had spent several hours watching this section of the border to make certain it wasn't mined. Then, sometime after midnight, he began his infiltration into Israel. He had been crawling for several minutes when he heard a guard call out, "Halt," in Yiddish.

Joseph replied in the same language saying he was a Jew who had been captured by the Lebanese and was trying to return to his home country. Four Israeli guards grabbed him, brought him back to their guardhouse, and questioned him for hours. He decided to change his story to the truth and told the guards he was a Mossad agent who had escaped from ISIS. They just laughed.

Fortunately, when their commander awoke the next morning, the guards took Joseph to him for further interrogation. Again, Joseph told his story and explained how he and his friend Aaron had been gone for two years on assignment for Mossad, had escaped ISIS in Syria, and had walked over four hundred miles to reach Israel.

The commander, a young captain from Jerusalem, knew several friends who worked for Mossad and called this information into them. In less than an hour, he received a reply telling him that his captive was indeed a Mossad agent, that he should be fed and clothed and shown every courtesy, and that a Mossad team would be joining him soon to take charge of Joseph.

47

OISHA HAVEL, CHIEF OF MOSSAD, Israel's national intelligence agency, watched the man sitting before him. He could not estimate the man's age. Captivity, torture, and almost two months of travel through the desert while being hunted by the enemy had taken their toll. Joseph Lieb was one of very few Israeli soldiers who had returned alive after being sent to infiltrate ISIS. The usual scenario was that burned and mutilated bodies of Israeli men who had been found to be spies by ISIS were dumped close to their country's border and left to rot until the Israelis found them.

"So, Joseph, you are well, relatively speaking?"

"Relatively, chief. A little sunburned and sick of eating lizards. But I am well. My Mossad brothers are helping me recover quickly. They got me very drunk two nights ago, and it was the best I've felt in two years."

"Good. Good. The coordinates you gave to our intelligence section have been checked. We verified them on our maps, and they do fall closely on the former village of Dabiq in Syria. We had to find an older map to even locate Dabiq. There was no previous indication that this was a major ISIS stronghold. We even checked the reliability of that small GPS you used, and it was within tolerances. One of our drones flew low over the area yesterday. It appears to be deserted. We could detect nothing, no signs of life, even with our infrared equipment—nothing at all. Our drone was not even fired upon."

Joseph nodded. "The base is the most well disguised I have ever seen. All of their assets are underground. I have not seen the secret areas of this base. Occasionally, I would bring supplies into the stronghold, but I was not allowed to go deeper into the facility. The men I worked with over two years whispered about the many underground activities, Chief. There are classrooms, a combat training center, a film studio, a large hospital, and a top-secret laboratory, which none of the laborers had ever seen. They only said they were told it was dangerous and that what it contained would provide victory for ISIS against the West and create a new Islamic world."

Havel had been chief of Mossad for over fifteen years. He had been stationed all over the world and had fought against the many enemies of Israel most of his life, even as a child in his kibbutz. This ISIS enemy was different, he thought. It was a revolution the likes of which he had never seen before. The ISIS soldiers they had captured and interrogated were well trained, dedicated, and disciplined. They were part of an offensive jihad like no other. Havel believed that ISIS fully intended to take over the entire Middle East and the world, if it could. The viral attacks that were underway may have been the beginning.

"Joseph, we have had other similar leaks over the years that confirm what you have told us. But we have never had coordinates before. Most of our people had no idea where they actually were in that vast desert." He paused for a moment. "Joseph, I assume you have heard of the ISIS viral attacks around the world."

"Yes, sir. I knew something was going to happen, but the use of viruses was a surprise."

"To all of us, my friend. Your arrival at this time with the coordinates of this secret underground base where these germs were most likely produced could not have been more opportune. Now we have a specific target to go after and destroy. Our nation and the world owe you a great debt. You and Aaron accomplished more than any other agents we have sent into ISIS territory over the years. In fact, we thought you had been murdered by these dogs long ago. It is a blessing that you have returned. I also want to tell you that you will be meeting with the prime minister to receive a special commendation. Your friend Aaron will receive the same, posthumously. Do you have family?"

"I have no wife, Chief, but my mother is still alive. And before I am returned to duty, I will visit her in our kibbutz, Neve Harif."

"Ah, Neve Harif. I know this kibbutz. It is one of our finest. It is a shame we cannot brag about your accomplishments publicly, Joseph. It would bring great honor to Neve Harif."

"Thank you, Chief. I knew and accepted those restrictions years ago when I was chosen to join Mossad. I have no complaints."

"Good. You may return to your unit, Joseph, and take as much time as you wish getting back to normal. Officially, I cannot condone your getting drunk again with your unit. But, unofficially, I can recommend it. Your service to Israel is immeasurable, and I thank you on behalf of our grateful nation."

The young man stood, saluted, and left the room.

And now, what do we do with this information? Havel thought. *Destroy this place in the desert, of course. But how and when? And what happens after that?*

He said a silent prayer and thanked God for men like Joseph and Aaron who had guided and protected and saved Israel for so many years. *Where do we get such men?* he wondered. *And how many more will die in our service.*

48

"GENERAL COLFAX, I UNDERSTAND THAT Acting President Akron has resigned and that Vice President Carson Dansby is now president. I tried to contact President Dansby with an update on our conversation of a few days ago, and your people told me he could not be reached and that I should communicate with you for the foreseeable future." The Israeli Prime Minister was concerned about the change in the American administration with the world at war.

"That's correct, Prime Minister. As you know, I was present during our previous discussion and can relay President Dansby's views. He is slightly indisposed but will be back on his feet very soon, I'm certain."

"Good, General. I know we are both busy in this time of war. But I wanted to speak to you about the coordinates we transmitted to you for an important ISIS base in Dabiq. I understand your forces have begun bombing the area. We believe it may be ISIS's main underground headquarters."

"Yes, Prime Minister. We began by flying one of our own drones over the coordinates as you did a few days before. Frankly, we saw nothing of interest. And our instruments detected nothing out of the ordinary. Nevertheless, we thoroughly bombed the area several times, at various hours, thinking we might catch them unawares or cause them to show themselves. We have found absolutely nothing."

"May I suggest that we continue our surveillance for a time, General Colfax? It may be that we must apply stronger armaments in order to bring about the desired result."

"Or, and I hate to say this, Mr. Prime Minister, but it may be that your agent, despite his best intentions, is simply mistaken."

"Perhaps, General. Perhaps. But I do not think so. I think this enemy hides well. And they hide so well because what they are hiding, I believe, is very special. And very dangerous. Let us simply continue to keep each other informed. And good luck to you and to President Dansby. Please give him my best wishes."

"I'll do that, Prime Minister. Thank you for your call and your good wishes. I'll pass them along." The two men hung up.

Prime Minister Shamir considered what his next action might be. All of his advisers recommended that Israel bring increased pressure on ISIS by beginning their own bombing campaign. They could use the American bunker buster bomb on the coordinates, but the prime minister was concerned that it would not be strong enough. The general had said that their own drone photography after their bombings showed no results. A red light and buzzer on his desk lit up suddenly, and a warning siren sounded loudly. He picked up his phone.

"Yes?"

"Mr. Prime Minister?"

"Yes. Is that you, Shavit?" It was Yitzhak Shavit, his chief of security.

"Yes, sir. We have received actionable intelligence that Jerusalem may experience an atomic weapon discharge within the next hour."

"Atomic? In Jerusalem? They wouldn't dare. This city is holy to Muslims as well as Jews."

"Nevertheless, Prime Minister, you should immediately leave your office for your bomb shelter beneath the Knesset in the Ben-Gurion complex. Members of the Knesset have already evacuated. The president has also been informed."

"All right, Shavit. I am on my way. Surely our defense forces can stop the aircraft."

"We are told an aircraft will not be part of the delivery system, Prime Minister, and our early warning radar system confirms this. It may be a smaller device, possibly one of the miniature drones being used by ISIS in other countries, which will be detonated perhaps by a cell phone or some other system. Our security people are on full alert for this possibility. Unfortunately, this drone flies at such a low altitude it cannot be picked up and destroyed by our Arrow missile defense system."

"God help us all, Shavit."

Shamir left his office and followed the guards' directions to the bomb shelter beneath the Knesset, the seat of the Israeli government. As he and many others were hurrying down the stairs to the shelter, the sound of a major explosion shook the building. Shamir knew this must be the first nuclear blast, one, he feared, of many. Many people screamed, and there was a total loss of power. Emergency lights came on quickly, and everyone continued down the stairs. There were no windows in the stairway area, and Shamir thought this was just as well since an atomic detonation may have blinded those who could see it.

Shamir had only been inside the bomb shelter once before, after he was sworn in as prime minister and was being shown some emergency procedures. He had complete office facilities in the shelter and passed old friends and other government officials as he found his way to his destination. Emergency lighting was in place throughout the basement. His secretary was already in his office, along with a large group of military men, including Yitzhak Shavit. He was on the phone and frantically making notes.

"Prime Minister, the shielded phones have just returned. I can confirm the attack was an atomic detonation, small yield, about a quarter mile from the Ben-Gurion complex. There are many casualties. We have captured the men, who have admitted they are ISIS agents. They are proud of what they have done. As we suspected, the bomb was delivered by a small drone, launched by one of the men from only a few hundred or so feet away. Our men saw what may have been the drone engine on fire. That could have protected us from a direct hit. Decontamination procedures are under way. That is all I know."

"Thank you, Shavit. Are the government ministers safe?"

"Most of them, as far as we can tell."

Moshe Rabin, chief of Staff of the Israeli armed forces, pushed his way into the office. "Prime Minister, I am glad you are safe. I know you will want to respond to this attack, and I am prepared to follow your orders."

"Good, Rabin. I have been wondering how we should change our tactics in bombing those new coordinates we received a few days ago from our agent who was imbedded with ISIS. Now I know. We will send one of our stealth bombers with that new weapon you and I have been discussing."

Rabin lowered his voice. "You mean the Sword of Ehud? Are you certain? Forgive me, Prime Minister, but it is my duty to repeat something you already know. We have understandings with the Americans that we will not use atomic weapons. This bomb we call the Sword of Ehud has a fifty-megaton yield and will penetrate every known concrete and steel fortification to a depth of one thousand feet. As you and I have discussed so many times, the use of an atomic weapon of this size, especially by Israel, could cause an escalation that would bring about a major change in warfare in the Middle East."

"Thank you, Rabin. Of course I am certain I must make this next move. And this decision is long overdue, in my opinion. The major change you mention has already been authorized by the Knesset in the event that we were ever attacked with an atomic weapon. Make the necessary arrangements. I want our military to respond as soon as possible."

49

ARNIE MASON WAS PLEASED. TO his surprise, Lucy had not become violently outraged at the announcement that Vice President Carson Dansby had just been sworn in as president after Rose Akron's resignation. It was their third day of forced togetherness, since neither one of them could leave his apartment during the military curfew due to the ISIS attack on Washington and possible radiation contamination.

True, Lucy had expressed her modest disappointment that the Supreme Court had ruled the interim election for president was null and void. After all, how could you replace an acting president with a new election when she was no longer in office?

Mason was grateful for two other things. First, he had begged off swearing in Carson Dansby and left that job to Justice Sara Lipman. He liked the sound of her New York accent, and she was pleased to be honored with this special assignment despite the wartime danger involved. It was too bad that there was no television coverage of the event because of the war footing the country was on. But photographers had taken plenty of shots of the videoconference swearing in for posterity. The second swearing in would have plenty of photography and other coverage, he was sure.

Sara had told him that President Dansby was still secluded in an unnamed location while Washington was presumed under continuing attack. The president looked poorly, she said, even given the fuzzy television transmission they used for the swearing in. Dansby admitted there had been an explosion near his quarters in an old home that was not sealed and protected against radiation or virus leaks. Apparently, he and his family had received radiation dosages, and a doctor was present now, treating them all.

But the new president's voice was strong enough, and the swearing in took place without incident. Mason thought Dansby would make a decent president and could also bring a little normalcy back to the capital now that Akron had resigned. The rivalry between the parties, as well as that between Tom Falkner and Lucy, should calm down too. With Rose Akron's departure, the interim election had been halted. God knew the country had a lot of healing to do.

Mason was also thankful he'd had enough forethought not to point out to Lucy that she had actually lost nothing, because polling showed her 47 percentage points behind Falkner in the interim election. Her defeat, if the election had continued, was a forgone conclusion.

Strange, though, how she had begun to smile. Lucy seldom showed approval in any way, let alone laughed. Mason couldn't think of any reason for her humor, but he did thank God she was in a good mood and open to his meager advances. He was very grateful.

"Arnie," she said. "We need to talk. I want your complete concentration. This is important."

Uh oh, Mason thought. *What have I done wrong now?*

"Arnie, how well do you know Carson Dansby?"

"How well? Why, we've seen each other around town many times over the years. He was senator from New Mexico for three terms before Rose Akron chose him for the vice presidency."

"I know all that. I mean, how well do you *really* know him?" Her smile had broadened.

Mason sensed danger in the way she posed the question and didn't want to lose her good mood. "I guess I don't know what you mean, love," he managed to say, hoping his reply was bland enough.

Jennings reached over the side of the bed into her ever-present handbag and pulled out a file. Mason had begun to hate those files! They always meant some kind of problem for him.

"What I mean, Justice Mason, is exactly this." Her smile was gone. "Did you know, for instance, that that clown Dansby wasn't even born in the United States? And did you know, Justice Mason, that that makes him ineligible to be president? Did you know that, Justice Mason?"

Mason swallowed hard. What was this all about? What did she mean? What was in the file?

"No, dear, I didn't know any of that." It was a lame reply, but he knew she was on the attack.

Jennings opened the file. "It turns out that our friend Dansby was actually born in Mexico, which, as I understand it, is *not* part of the United States." Her voice rose as she spat out the words. "*Therefore, he is not eligible to be president and never should have been sworn in!* Hell, he never should have been sworn in as vice president. Now, what do you say, Mr. Justice Mason?"

Arnie realized he didn't have much time to come up with a reply that wouldn't enrage her. And he reminded himself that this paradise he had been enjoying could be lost very quickly. "If this is true, my dear, and I don't doubt you for a moment, a major travesty has been done to the United States. Uh, in a time of war."

"Exactly. *Exactly!* Now, what are you going to do about it?"

"Well, the court will have to wait for a legal challenge before we—"

"The challenge is already on your desk. My attorneys drafted it and submitted it today while you and I were—busy—here in your apartment."

"Good. That's excellent, Lucy. Good thinking on your part. We'll get to the bottom of this, I promise you. Over the next few weeks, I'll—"

"Next few weeks, my ass," she fumed. "You and your can't-be-fired jackass justices will take it up *tomorrow*. Do you understand me, Arnie? *Tomorrow.*"

"Yes, dear. Of course I understand you. Tomorrow it will be. I'll call my secretary now and send her your notes so she can prepare some preliminary materials for our discussion. We'll probably still be forced to meet by videoconference, but we can get the job done."

"There better be a lot more than just discussion, Arnie—*a lot* more. If Dansby isn't thrown out of office quickly by your decision, you'll never see me again. And I mean any *part* of me," she said.

50

"LADIES AND GENTLEMEN, I'D LIKE you to come to order, please. Thank you for meeting by videoconference. I'm told that we should be able to leave our homes soon and bring our business back to the Supreme Court facilities. We have a critical issue before us today in the form of an emergency appeal from former House Speaker Lucy Jennings, claiming that President Carson Dansby should never have been sworn in as president because he was not born in this country. I see a copy of her appeal was also released to the press, so we ought to come up with something intelligent to say about it. Let's begin our discussion. Justice Cordero, why don't you start us off?"

"Arnie, may I have a moment before Vince begins?" It was Sara Lipman.

"Of course, Sara."

"I think you all know that I was honored to have sworn in President Dansby the other day. What I didn't say publicly at the time was that he was suffering from radiation illness. His office called me today. Apparently, the ISIS people did not know Dansby was in the area, and the nuclear blast was set off by accident just outside his secret residence. His entire family received what I was told today was serious exposure to radiation. He's been under a doctor's care, and that is continuing. That's all I know."

The justices took a moment to share stories about President Dansby and wish him well.

"Thank you, Sara. Please keep us informed if you hear any more. The last thing this country needs right now is more instability in its leadership. Justice Cordero, will you continue our former discussion, please?"

Cordero had been on the Supreme Court bench for twelve years. He was a longtime, intimate friend of Senate Majority Leader and would-be United States President Tom Falkner. Breaking an unwritten rule for Supreme Court justices, he had openly campaigned for Falkner in two elections and was widely outspoken in his praise for the senator. Unbeknownst to Chief Justice Mason, Cordero had also slept with Lucy Jennings and was jealous of the chief's current liaison with what Cordero referred to as "the best piece of ass in Washington, DC."

"Chief, I think this is easily solved. I don't think former Speaker Jennings has standing before the court, and we should ignore her appeal."

Several justices nodded in agreement. But upstart Justice Wigginton raised his hand to be recognized. Mason wanted to ignore him, but he was temporarily stunned by what Cordero had suggested. Technically speaking—and everything the court examined was considered highly technical—Lucy Jennings was out of office and very well might not have standing. Mason said a silent prayer that he would never have to tell her that to her face.

"Yes, Justice Wigginton."

"Thank you, Chief. In the materials faxed to us on this matter, I see that Speaker Jennings is claiming that she, and all citizens of the United States, will be irreparably injured if current President Dansby is not removed from office because he was born to American parents in Mexico, if that's a fact. As you and all of my brethren on the court know, any citizen can bring suit before this court claiming injury if some perceived action is not corrected. In this case, Speaker Jennings points out that, if Dansby is not eligible to be president, every action he takes, every bill he signs could cause injury to all American citizens because every one of Dansby's acts would be illegal. I think this gives her standing and meets the criteria for our consideration."

Mason began to think more highly of the relatively young man. Perhaps he wasn't the asshole his fellow justices said he was.

"A good point, Justice Wigginton. Yes, Justice Cobbins?"

It was Harley Cobbins again, with his often folksy, always off-color remarks. It was rumored that Cobbins had actually memorized every word of the Constitution and all of its amendments and could speak for hours on any one of them. Mason hoped that was not going to happen now.

"Arnie, this is just more of the apparently never-ending bullshit we've been hearing on the court and in the country lately. Let me remind my brothers and sisters on the court about the history of this issue. First of all, it has never before been brought before the Supreme Court. In fact, it has never been tested legally at any judicial level. I submit there's a damn good reason for that. The Constitution does require that, to be eligible for the presidency, one must be a natural born citizen of the United States. Trouble is, those good ol' founding fathers never defined what 'natural born' means. We used to believe that language in this country meant what it said. Natural born means born here on the dirt of the United States. Seems simple, don't it?

"Well, some of these fancy so-called constitutional lawyers have— excuse me, ladies—fucked up the simple meaning of simple words."

Justice Lipman grinned. Wigginton was red faced.

Cobbins wasn't finished by a long shot. "As if we don't have enough of these yellow dog, constitutional lawyers to translate simple English for us, we have a lardload of overpaid university scholars who also have opinions. Some people on this court have held those university positions"—he glared at Wigginton—"before they were, well, elevated to join the supremes. You'd think they would have cleaned up their act. The law requires that, to be a natural born US citizen, you have to be one 'at the moment of birth.' Scholars say that means born of United States citizens, regardless of where in damnation they were at the time. We've always accepted that. And, as I say, it has never been challenged.

"Truth is, the matter has never been settled. Every president we've had, good or bad, was either a citizen at the adoption of the Constitution in 1789 or born in the United States; of those in the latter group, seven presidents had parents who were not US citizens. Here's another good example. You'll recall when Senator John McCain ran for president. I voted for him, by the way. Would have made a damn good president.

"John was a navy brat. His dad was a navy officer stationed in the Panama Canal Zone during some of our glory years when this country actually kept its possessions instead of giving them away for nothing. Well, McCain, through no fault of his own, was born while his American parents were living in the Zone. Now, some idiot challenged his natural born citizenship in a lower court during the campaign, and the challenge was thrown out. We all knew and understood that any kid born to people in the military was as natural born as any other citizen. That's always been the case."

"But, Justice Cobbins—" It was Wigginton again.

"Just hold your horses, young Wigginton. You have a lot to learn, and I can't teach all of it to you in just this one tirade. You will all also recall Mitt Romney running for president. Hell, he was born in Michigan, but some bozo pointed out that his father, George Romney, who also ran for president, was born in Mexico to American parents living there on business, so that should make Mitt ineligible to run. Where the hell is the logic in that? Just horseshit on top of bullshit. President Dansby's parents were American citizens too, so the same reasoning and precedent applies to him.

"Now, I wasn't even going to bring up the Obama situation. But, if I don't, that wiseass new Justice Wigginton will say something about it. To refresh your memories, a whole bunch of folks got together when Obama ran and claimed he was born in Kenya, not Hawaii. So Obama got an official copy of his birth certificate and published it, verified by the Hawaii Department of Health. What the hell else could you ask for? Some dimwits claimed all those records were forgeries. I said at the time that it was their brains that were forgeries.

"Here's my final thought about this happy horseshit, Arnie. A few more of these fancy-ass experts have suggested that the precise meaning of the natural-born-citizen clause shouldn't even be decided by the courts because it's truly a political question, not a legal question. I agree. It's obvious to any ordinary fool, with no legal training at all, that the issue should be decided by Congress, if they can ever pull their heads out of their asses long enough to act responsibly about any goddamned thing. And that's where I think this nonissue stands. I say, if this needs to be further defined and spelled out, let Congress do it. That's where it belongs." Cobbins pulled a filthy handkerchief out of his breast pocket, blew his nose, and then wiped his face.

The members of the court were silent, most of them smiling after Cobbins's combination of tongue-lashing and diatribe. They waited for the chief justice to say something.

"Well," Mason finally muttered, thinking he had seen Lucy Jennings for the last time. "Justice Cobbins, if there are no objections, I'm going to ask you to draw up a statement for the court to release to the press along the lines of your general remarks this morning, stating that the court will not take up this emergency petition. You might try to eliminate a few of those 'horseshits' and 'bullshits,' just so it sounds legal. Oh, I wouldn't mind at all if you left in that part about it being Congress's business, not ours, minus that part about them having their heads up their asses."

"Actually, I liked that part," Sara Lipman said.

"So did I," Mason replied. "This informal meeting is adjourned."

51

FORMER ACTING PRESIDENT ROSE AKRON finished shaking hands with the staff that had accompanied her into the protected bunker beneath the White House. She waited until she received a message that Vice President Dansby had been sworn in, but she was concerned about the report that he had received a dose of radiation. Dansby's doctors told her they didn't know how serious his condition was and didn't want to move him to an area hospital because of the attacks around the city. The medical equipment in his secure location had limited value.

"Madam President, I hate to see you go." It was Sherm Boyle, her chief of staff who had been with her since her election to the House and then through her term as Speaker and, finally, during her selection as acting president by the Congress.

"We've discussed this, Sherm. I waited until I thought I had done all I could do and the presidency was secure. My last reports indicate that the attacks in the capital have stopped and that our decontamination protocols are working. I'm glad I was in the presidency when the virus thing was resolved. Now, I'm certain I need to get out of the way and let Carson Dansby handle things without me hanging around."

"So, what are you going to do? I mean, shouldn't we have some kind of ceremony or something?"

Akron touched her friend's arm. "Sherm, even if it were possible in this situation, which it isn't, I've had quite enough of these ceremonies over the past eighteen months. It was never something I liked or wanted. It's over. And now I just want to get back to my family."

Boyle frowned. "I know what you mean. It's just a damn shame that they wouldn't give you a chance—I mean a real chance."

Akron shook her head. "Oh, I think they did, Sherm. It turns out that no one liked the idea of an acting president and damn few people even knew about the constitutional amendment that authorized one. When the Congress passed the Twenty-Eighth Amendment a few weeks ago calling for an interim election, most of the states and the people seemed to think it was a good idea. Hell, I only saw a half dozen editorials opposing it, and they were halfhearted."

"Still, I have a feeling they'll miss you before too long."

"Well, I'd like to say that I'll miss them, but I won't. I will miss you, though, Sherm. You've been loyal and dependable, and I'll never forget you."

They shook hands and then hugged.

"So, when are you going home?"

"Right now, as soon as the air force tells me we're all clear. They can send whatever I've left in my office and the personal stuff in the White House back home to Duluth. Sherm, I know you'll help out President Dansby all you can, and I thank you for that."

"Rose." It was the only time Boyle had used her first name since she had been named acting president. "Rose, it's been an honor to serve with you."

"And with you, Sherm. At least we accomplished one thing."

"What's that?"

"We didn't get impeached."

52

AJOR ARI BICKLER HAD FLOWN in the Israeli Air Force for nineteen years. His original pilot training had been with the United States Air Force in Columbus, Mississippi. After completing that program, he'd returned to Israel and had flown F-15 and F-16 fighters on many secret combat missions into Syria, Lebanon, Egypt, Iran, and Iraq. He was the most experienced and most highly decorated pilot in Israeli history.

Two years ago, he'd returned to the United States and trained in a top secret version of their new stealth aircraft, the F-35 fighter-bomber. The F-35 carried traditional high explosive bombs and missiles and could quickly be converted to atomic weapons if needed. On his return to Israel, he had taken command of a new squadron of F-35s, which had been covertly modified to carry an Israeli-made, fifty-megaton atomic bomb. While the Israelis had had atomic weapons for many years, they were of a smaller yield and had never been used in combat. The construction of the bomb and the modification to the aircraft was done in secret, with no notification to the American government. The events in the Middle East and the rise of ISIS had convinced the Israelis that they should prepare for any eventuality. They could inform the United States of their use of atomic weapons if that ever came about.

Major Bickler came to attention and saluted as Prime Minister Ehud Shamir and Deputy Air Force General Avihu Ben Amir entered the room. Bickler had no specific idea why he had been ordered to report to these men in Tel Aviv, but he suspected he would be charged with an important mission and was eager to receive his orders. General Ben Amir was well known for being straightforward and a man of few words.

"At ease, Bickler," General Ben Amir said. "You are aware that our nation has been attacked with a nuclear weapon by ISIS forces?"

"Yes, sir."

"The prime minister and I wish to speak to you about a top secret mission you are to undertake. Everything you see and hear in this room is also top secret and should never be repeated or discussed. Do you understand?"

"Yes, sir."

The general pressed a switch, and a detailed map of Syria appeared on a large screen. "I'm sure you recognize this country, Bickler. Your file says you have visited it many times."

"I can neither confirm nor deny that information, General," Bickler said with a smile.

"Excellent. Tomorrow at exactly 0200, you will depart Tel Aviv. You will fly north over the Mediterranean at low altitude and enter Syrian airspace at the coastal city of Latakia. At that point, you will climb to fifty thousand feet and fly to specific coordinates that will be given to you in your detailed briefing and entered into your GPS bombing platform. Upon reaching those coordinates, your weapon, an A-555 atomic device better known as 'the Sword of Ehud,' will be armed and released. Once the weapon is dropped, you will immediately depart Syrian airspace and return to base. When you leave here this morning, you will report to your squadron for a more detailed briefing. Do you have any questions?"

"Sir, will I have any fighter cover during the mission?"

"No. As you are aware, the F-35 has stealth protection, and you have already flown many training missions in the aircraft, more than any other Israeli pilot. There is no practical Syrian Air Force still in existence. Russian missiles are within range of your target, but your electronic countermeasures can easily avoid them. These Russian weapons are vastly inferior to your stealth equipment. We want and expect this mission to be completed with no identification by any country. You have also practiced dropping simulated mock weapons of the identical size and weight of the Ehud."

"And will I be the only aircraft assigned to this mission?"

"Yes. Any other questions?"

"No, sir."

"Mr. Prime Minister, do you have any questions or statements for Major Bickler?"

"Just that your country is depending on you, Bickler. Your successful mission may stop the cruelest and most vicious enemy we have ever faced. God be with you."

53

PRESIDENT CARSON DANSBY WAS TOO weak to raise his head or return the salute of Interim Joint Chiefs Chairman Dixie Colfax. Dansby's longtime doctor and personal friend, Skip Donner, stood beside the hospital bed, his fingers on the president's wrist.

"Mr. President, I just want to inform you that we have apprehended the men who bombed the Capitol and the Pentagon with viral weapons, as well as another enemy team that detonated a low-level nuclear device close to your quarters. Apparently, you were not a target. Our military was closing in on an ISIS team, and they panicked and detonated their bomb with no knowledge of your location. They are in custody and are being interrogated. Although they appear to be Americans, they have already confessed to being ISIS agents."

Dansby's voice could barely be heard. "Good work, General. Thank you. How is my family?"

"They have been taken to Washington University hospital, Mr. President. Their prognosis is excellent."

The president tried to smile. "Thanks again, General."

The general saluted. "Sir," he said and left the room.

Outside, General Colfax saw several officers he recognized, including most of the Joint Chiefs. The president's chief of staff was present, and a few senators and members of the House.

"How bad is he, Dixie?"

Colfax shook his head. "The doctor told me before I went into his room that they don't expect him to last much longer. He got a hell of a dose of radiation. So did most members of his family and his staff, but they're doing better than he is. Tom Barrington over there"—Colfax gestured to the young man on the phone—"I think you know the president's chief of staff? Barrington got a dose, too, but the docs say he'll be okay. Just pretty sick for a while. It may sound stupid to say this, but I guess we're lucky this was a low-yield nuke. The hell of it is that these jokers who set off the blast were on their way to another location and had no idea they were close to the vice president's hidden site. They panicked when they saw our military approaching and set off the bomb."

Barrington hung up the phone and rubbed his hands vigorously over his face and head. "General Colfax, may I see you, please?"

"Sure, Tom. What is it?"

Barrington just stared at him for a moment. "Sir, that was Sherm Boyle on the phone. President Akron's helicopter is down."

"What? What do you mean—down?"

"That's all they know right now, sir. The copter was taking her to a safe airstrip to fly her back to Duluth. They don't know if it was engine trouble or if they were hit by some kind of weapon. There are no reports yet about ... survivors."

Colfax shook his head. "Jesus Christ, is that poor woman ever going to get a break? Stay on this, will you, Tom? Let me know when you hear something."

"Yes, sir, I will."

Air Force General Chuck Clark didn't want to ask the question he had on his mind, but he took a deep breath and cleared his throat. "Dixie, maybe this isn't the time to bring this up, but I feel like we have to. If—when the president—ah, when he passes away, what do we do?"

"What do you mean, Chuck?"

"Well, who's next in line? Who's the next president? Dansby didn't have time to choose his own VP. And even if he did, the Senate didn't have time to confirm. The whole Congress is scattered all over. We don't know how many of them survived the viral and atomic attacks. Truth is, we don't even know if we have a government right now. We need to be prepared."

"I agree, Chuck. The next in line would be the Speaker of the House Dante Caruso."

"He's dead." It was General Cort Timmons, another of the Joint Chiefs. "The virus got him early. I just confirmed it."

"Great, that makes it the president pro tempore of the Senate, if my knowledge of succession is right. Who is that?"

One of the senators in the room spoke up. "It's Karl Doherty. Or it was. The virus got him too. I think that means the secretary of state is next."

"Also gone, I'm afraid." It was one of the representatives in the room. "He was in the Speaker's office below the Capitol, where many House members got a lethal dose of radiation. Apparently, there was a bad leak in their underground facility. I've been warning for years that the basement in that old building would never stand up under stress, much less a nuclear bomb. I was told that several walls crumbled after the detonation. So, if the secretary of state is gone, what the hell do we do now?"

"I used to have all this stuff memorized." It was Tom Barrington, the president's chief of staff. He had just come back from the bathroom after another attack of radiation poisoning hit him hard. "My memory isn't too good right now, but I believe the secretary of the Treasury follows state. She's next. That's Robin Slater."

"Oh, Jesus," one of the Joint Chiefs shouted. "That's just what we need—another woman president with no experience. Robin Slater was appointed by former President Danzig because she worked on his campaign in Ohio. She doesn't know shit."

Colfax cleared his throat. "That doesn't matter. We follow the line of succession through the president's cabinet until we locate someone who can serve. Does anyone know where Secretary Slater is?"

There was silence in the room.

"Tom, will you try to locate her, please? Does anyone have a copy of the line of succession? This may take a while."

No one spoke.

"Well, we can get a copy somewhere. That would be our next step. Maybe if the Internet is working."

"Dixie, there is another option." It was General Chuck Clark again. "What's that, Chuck?"

"Understand that I'm just bringing this up as a sort of last resort, you might say. Before he died, Clint Courier had drawn up a plan for the Joint Chiefs to take over if the acting president was … uh … unable to carry out her duties. All the Joint Chiefs are here. We could put that plan into effect, if you agree."

"Let me get this straight, Chuck. You're suggesting that we carry out a military takeover of the United States. Is that right?"

"I wouldn't put it quite that way, Dixie. This would be a temporary thing until we can get the line of succession in place. Or—"

"Or what, Chuck?"

"Or until we get this damned war under control." Clark was getting angrier.

"Or maybe until we get this or that or the other accomplished, huh? Is that what this is all about?" Colfax was raising his voice.

The door to the president's room opened, and his doctor came out. "I'm afraid he's gone, gentlemen. The president has just passed."

"Jesus Christ," someone said.

"Holy shit," said another.

"Dixie, we have to do something." It was Chuck Clark again. "The fact is, no one is in charge, and no one knows where to find anyone who could take over. I say it's up to us."

Colfax shook his head. "I won't be a party to a military takeover. This is America, not some goddamned third world country where the military does whatever it damn well pleases. It's a simple rule. We follow the Constitution in war and peace."

"Dixie, all Chuck is saying is, in the absence of a successor to the president, we may have to step in and take charge." It was Admiral Cort Timmons. "We just can't let things drift. There's a war on, for God's sake. American cities have been attacked. Thousands have been killed. Our citizens are panicking. Our allies are worse off than we are. We have to show some leadership and strength."

"I still say we wait and try to locate someone in succession and take it from there." Colfax was adamant.

"Dixie, even if we wait, there's a good chance that whoever we find to replace the president would have no idea how to run a government at war. At least the Joint Chiefs can handle that part."

Colfax came to attention. "Gentlemen, I'm chairman of the Joint Chiefs, appointed by President Rose Akron and confirmed by the Senate. I'm also your superior officer. I'm telling you to forget this idea and stand down."

Chuck Clark had an old Army Colt .45 in his uniform pocket. He drew it out, pointing it at the floor.

"Dixie, you and I have known each other for a lot of years. We've fought together and gotten drunk together. I'm not going to point this weapon at you, but I'm asking you to step aside. The rest of the Joint Chiefs are with me."

Colfax glanced around the room and saw nods of agreement from the other chiefs. "Chuck, there are members of the House and Senate and half a dozen other officers in this room listening to you. What you propose is illegal and unlawful and against everything America stands for. You're a better man than this."

"Maybe that would work in the old America, Dixie, but these are different times. We haven't had a real president since that woman was appointed acting president. Our government has been attacked, and our president has just died. We don't even know if we have enough living members of the House and Senate to conduct business. Same goes for the cabinet and the succession thing. And what about the ISIS agents in this country we haven't found yet? We could have more attacks at any moment. It's time to take action to protect this country, and we'd be violating our own oaths if we didn't take charge."

Clark walked over to the main doorway, opened it, and motioned to the two guards to come into the room. "Sergeant, I am placing General Colfax under house arrest. Please take him into custody, keep him under guard, and show him every courtesy. This will all be explained later."

54

MAJOR ARI BICKLER COMPLETED HIS preflight check of the Israeli F-35 and admired the blackened aircraft for a moment. He had never flown a better one. A special weapons crew had gone over the A-555 atomic bomb, which they'd nicknamed the Ehud, and had made certain it would operate correctly. The bomb release mechanism had also been tested several times, and the target coordinates had been entered into the bombing computer. Bickler had complete confidence in his aircraft and his equipment.

His full briefing had been short and sweet. The entire flight would last only slightly over an hour, barring any enemy contact. This was not expected. If his aircraft was not able to make the return flight, he was given ditching instructions. Several Israeli surface vessels would be waiting for him off the coast of Tel Aviv. Otherwise, special landing instructions back at his base would be followed, where his aircraft and he, himself, would be checked for radiation exposure and decontaminated if necessary.

The only previous detonation of a fifty-megaton atomic weapon had been an experiment at the hands of the Russians. The weapon had been detonated in the Pacific Ocean during the Cold War in the 1960s to frighten the United States and its allies. The Russians had never released any data about the explosion or its aftermath. While scientists had given their estimates, the truth was that no one really knew what might occur after a nuclear explosion of this size. None of this mattered to Bickler. He had flown many combat missions during his career and had been shot at and shot down on several occasions. He had no concerns; he was totally concentrated on the mission.

At precisely 0200, Bickler applied power to the single-engine F-35, climbed immediately to twenty thousand feet and then headed over the Mediterranean and descended to five hundred feet, as per his orders and the flight plan. His full complement of stealth equipment, a supplement to the aircraft's stealth configuration itself, was fully functional. In addition, his early warning electronic countermeasures were operating normally. He and his aircraft were ready.

Even at his low altitude of five hundred feet, Bickler's radar could pick up the Syrian city of Latakia, where he was to cross into Syrian territory and climb to fifty thousand feet. He did so and was pleased again at how swiftly and smoothly the F-35 soared to his bombing altitude. He double-checked the bombing coordinates in the computer. The weather was perfect, and his defense systems had not picked up any enemy radars or weapons that might be tracking him. He did not expect any but thought the Russian missiles the Syrian government had dispersed around the area might possibly be able to identify his aircraft. Still, the F-35s stealth equipment had proven superior to Russian radars the Israelis had captured and tested, so Bickler had little to concern him as he approached the target coordinates.

His briefing officers had told him not to expect any target signatures on his radar. He would be bombing a specific set of coordinates that would not reflect on his equipment. He set his bombing mechanism to fully automatic and approached the coordinates. Should any of his equipment fail, he was prepared to manually release the weapon on time, on target.

The sound of his bomb bay doors opening and the green "go" lights told him all automatic functions were working perfectly. He felt the F-35 surge slightly as the huge bomb was released. He turned immediately toward the Mediterranean Sea again and maintained fifty thousand feet altitude. Bickler had studied scientific descriptions of what to expect at detonation, but this new weapon was an unknown. While there was always the chance that he and his aircraft would be disintegrated in the blast, he thought that was only a faint possibility.

The bomb had been set to explode below ground. The Israelis wanted the weapon to penetrate deep below the surface of the coordinates to make certain they would engage and destroy all enemy troops and weapons and whatever else was hidden underground.

As Bickler reached the coast, he waited for some sign of the detonation. Even if the weapon had reached its maximum depth, he expected some blast wave or flash of light. He checked his time from target and expected detonation time, and they had both passed. His warning systems were all working perfectly and detected no radiation at even the lowest levels. All systems were still operational.

He cursed at what he assumed was a bombing malfunction and called in to his base with the coded response that let them know what had happened. Over water, he descended to five hundred feet for the return flight to Tel Aviv. He would be on the ground again in just a few minutes.

55

"THE AMERICANS ARE RESPONSIBLE FOR this." Russian President Dimitri Obloff pounded his desk, knocking over a large glass of vodka.

"But, Mr. President, they have been attacked too. Their government is in much the same disarray as ours. And they have sent us the vaccine they have developed against the ISIS virus."

"It will poison us if we use it, Alexei. Can't you see? This is the perfect opportunity for the cursed Americans to invade us without using their military. First the virus and then the atomic weapons. Now the so-called cure for the virus. It is one thing after another. We must respond. We still have our missiles."

"But, Dimitri, there is no proof that the Americans have been a part of this. And the viral attack has crippled our military, including our missile crews. We cannot respond that way. I should also say that the Americans cannot use their own missiles for the very same reason."

Obloff kicked his desk and poured himself more vodka. "It is that damned woman in the White House, Alexei. That would never happen in Russia. It takes a man to lead a country." He swallowed the vodka. "There must be something we can do."

There was a knock on the president's office door. A general entered with several papers, saluted, placed them on Obloff's desk, saluted again, and left the room.

"Now she is gone, Alexi. The American president has resigned. After drawing us all into war and contaminating all of our countries, she has left to continue her knitting." He threw the papers on the floor and poured more vodka.

"This may be good for us, Mr. President. We have many spies within the American government. Perhaps it may be time to make a move against them while they have no leader. Even their General Courier succumbed to the virus."

"Yes. Yes. At least something good has come out of this mess. Contact our agents—if we can still communicate in any way. Tell them to form a plan. I don't care how radical it is. This is a time to be radical. There may yet be a way to thwart these Yankee dogs."

56

THERE WAS NO WARNING WHEN the Israeli bomb struck the coordinates of ISIS's underground headquarters. Bakr and Ali were several levels below ground in a Quran class, alternately listening to the teaching of the imam and praying with the rest of the men. Bakr had not heard from many of his attack teams recently and was growing nervous.

Of course, they did hear the bomb pierce the earth above them and crash into the underground compound. This did not create any blast since the bomb was set to penetrate up to a thousand feet before it produced its nuclear detonation. The weapon actually penetrated only five hundred feet, which took it down to the fourth level of the compound, stopping inside a wall adjacent to the atomic and viral laboratories. There it rested. There was no detonation. The bomb had not been configured or dropped improperly. Nor had it been damaged in any way. It was in perfect condition, except that it did not explode.

"The Americans must be dropping weapons again, Ali," Bakr said to his friend. "Obviously, they are guessing once more about our location. This bomb was not successful despite their million-dollar equipment and aircraft. Come, let us find what exactly has occurred and see if we need to take any further precautions."

The two men left the classroom, and Bakr immediately called security on his cell phone.

They moved to the nearest elevator but were told by a guard that the system was not operating properly. He opened the door for them to the adjacent stairs, and they descended one level to the science laboratories.

"The Americans were fortunate enough to disturb our power supply for a short time, Ali. Repairs are underway, and we will be back to normal before too long."

They walked down a corridor and could see a crowd of guards standing beside a crushed wall. As they drew closer, they saw the outline of a large bomb inside the wall.

"Is there anyone here who can tell us the nature of this bomb?" Bakr asked.

A man in a white coat, who Ali had previously seen in a science lab, stepped forward and saluted Bakr. "My Caliph, as you can see this bomb is quite large—the largest we have examined. From a brief investigation of the nose and the reinforced metal casing, I can tell you that it has significant penetrating capabilities, which is proven by its ability to reach this level of our quarters with no apparent damage to the weapon. It must have been dropped from a very high altitude. Our best estimate now is that it is a larger version of the so-called American bunker buster bomb. We have not yet tried to move it since we do not know its exact nature. The Americans are famous for including delaying mechanisms in their weapons. There are markings on the side we cannot see clearly, which may explain its origin and give us more information. Other men are coming with instruments that may be able to discover the bomb's contents. With respect, my Caliph, although I know that Allah, bless his holy name, protects you at all times, I implore you to retire to some safe location until we have disarmed this weapon." He saluted again and stepped back.

Bakr and Ali got as close as they could to the bomb. "An excellent analysis, Zayrus. Thank you. Please continue to proceed with caution and keep me informed."

"I will do so, my Caliph." The man saluted yet again and went back to his examination.

"Come, Ali. There is nothing we can do here for the moment. And Allah continues to protect us, holding back any power this bomb may have. Let us return to the shelter. I want to try again to communicate with my commanders in other sectors. Then I will order some refreshment and company, and we may find something else to amuse us."

57

ARNIE MASON SAT ALONE IN his apartment. Lucy Jennings was
gone. For good. There was no note. She never would have taken
the time to leave a note. It was just over.

Mason had known this would happen as soon as they'd heard of Carson
Dansby's death. President—that office was the one thing Lucy coveted
more than anything else in her life. She certainly wanted it more than her
relationship with Arnie Mason. A chief justice just wasn't enough for her.

Mason thought over what she had gone through in her attempts to
get that illusive prize. She'd had a bill passed through the House when
she was still Speaker recommending her to the Joint House-Senate
Committee that would choose an acting president. The bill had never
passed the Senate, which had adjourned during the previous election.
Then Lucy had been defeated for her House seat in that election. But
that hadn't so much as slowed her down. She'd worked for months
behind the scenes on her next scheme.

That's when she'd brought Arnie Mason—Supreme Court Chief
Justice Arnold Mason—into her life. Widowed, still immature where
women were concerned, Mason had been, quite literally, knocked off his
feet when Lucy had knocked on the door of his apartment. Her lawyers
had drafted a proposed Twenty-Eighth Amendment to the Constitution
calling for an interim election for president, which would effectively
remove Acting President Rose Akron. Lucy had brought Arnie into her
plan to support the amendment, and he had fallen for it—rather, had
fallen for her—completely.

When Akron had resigned and the Supreme Court had declared the interim election null and void because there was no longer an acting president, Lucy had still never slowed down, despite the fact that the United States was now at war with ISIS. When Vice President Carson Dansby was sworn in as President, she'd never blinked, petitioning the court to have him removed because she said he wasn't a natural born citizen. But there was no proof of that and no legal rulings at any level to support her claim. By any previous standard, Dansby was as much a citizen as any other American. She had lost again, but you'd never know it.

Dansby had died from radiation poisoning delivered by an ISIS bomb. Lucy was the only one Arnie knew who'd actually celebrated Dansby's death. She'd run around Arnie's apartment applauding and laughing. That night had been their last one together, and he remembered it vividly. She's sat alone in the living room for a long time, drinking scotch. Then she'd started packing. It hadn't taken her long. He'd begged her to stop and come to bed. But he had known it was all over. The next morning, she was gone.

So, what would she do now? What was her plan? Arnie was no longer of use to her; that was clear. But he knew she would never give up. Not Lucy. She would work out yet another nefarious scheme to get what she wanted, no matter the consequences. Who or what would it be? Who would the man, or woman, be who she next chose to help her get the grand prize—the presidency?

Mason took a deep breath and made a resolution to move on with his life, pour himself into the court and its work, and make up for the time he had squandered on Lucy Jennings. Yes, he loved her. Yes, he would never forget her. Yes, it was true that a man like him would never have had a chance for a moment with a woman like Lucy under normal circumstances. So, why not count his blessings and get on with his work? And good luck to the next poor bastard who couldn't give her what she wanted. Mason poured himself a drink. Scotch. Neat. Just as Lucy Jennings would have wanted.

58

"IT COULD BE THE DIFFERENCE in atmospheric pressure, Prime Minister, complicated by the unknown structures penetrated by the bomb after it entered the earth. We have been working on every possible reason for the lack of detonation and that is our only logical explanation."

"Sir?" It was Ari Bickler, the pilot. "I know that we have another bomb—another Ehud. Surely our scientists can modify this second bomb so that I can release it again to get the expected nuclear explosion."

"Prime Minister?"

"Yes, Dr. Reisen." Eighty-three-year-old Dr. Marcus Reisen was the head of the Israeli nuclear weapons development program. Since the age of thirty-nine, he had created every one of his country's major nuclear weapons systems. Israel had never admitted to having a nuclear program, so Reisen's official public title sounded very academic and obscure. There was nothing obscure about him—odd perhaps but not obscure. A bit frail and stooped now in his rumpled, gray suit, a ring of snow-white hair around his head, Reisen's pale blue eyes still shown with vitality, as they had in his youth. So did his mind.

"If I may. I'm sure that the explanation given by our technicians is correct as far as it goes. I have worked on the Ehud for several years. It is like another of my children. Inside this weapon are many new techniques and improvements and also a few toys for the child to play with. And on the outside, the modern metallurgic casing has never been used before on a weapon of this type. No one knows what dropping a bomb of this size from fifty thousand feet into an unknown environment can do to a weapon. Most of all, we do not know what our enemy's reaction to it may be. Perhaps this enemy may become curious about this child of ours—too curious.

"During Ehud's construction, we placed many fail-safe systems inside its childlike brain. One thing may not work as well as we wish, but another may substitute. If it is still in one piece, and I feel certain it is, I suggest we have patience with the Ehud. Again, think of it as our child, our delicate new child. It was born into an uncertain world, into an unknown environment." Dr. Reisen looked pensive and scratched his beard.

"Perhaps this child is only taking its time before it decides to do what it has been told to do. Children are like that. Ehud may be looking over the new toys we placed inside its body. We all know how children can be. Sometimes they are stubborn. They must be coaxed. And these new toys I am telling you about can do the coaxing. What significant difference can it make to us and to the world if the Ehud explodes now or an hour from now? If it does not respond, we can always send them another child who is not as stubborn. But give this one some time. I think our child will start to play its game very soon."

The prime minister admired Dr. Reisen a great deal. They had been friends for half a century, and Reisen had never failed in his creation of new weapons. When he spoke of his "child" and his "toys," the Prime Minister had come to understand and have confidence in this man. As he said, what difference could a few hours make?

"Gentlemen, here is what we will do. We will proceed with all caution to make ready the second Ehud. Major Bickler, you will get some rest in preparation for a possible second mission. And, as Dr. Reisen has suggested, we will wait for our child to make up its mind."

59

THE ISIS TECHNICIANS WORKED CAREFULLY around the huge bomb that had penetrated their underground headquarters. They were no beginners at the task. For years, they had disarmed many different types of weapons, most of them American made, on battlefields throughout the Middle East. They were most concerned about America's inclination to place delaying fuses and trick mechanisms inside many of their bombs, in hopes of catching the enemy by surprise, even hours after a bombing raid was over, when the apparatus would finally explode.

This experience on the battlefield had given ISIS critical knowledge about where to find these delaying components and how to disarm them. The technicians had not yet tried to move or even touch this bomb. That was the first rule of disarming such a weapon. A team of seven highly experienced men had photographed it from every available angle and compared it to pictures of American bombs they had seen and worked on before. It was like nothing else they had ever confronted. Their catalogues of British and French bombs, used infrequently during the war, were also checked with no result. The metal casing itself was of a type they had never seen before.

Finally, the decision was made to use a fluoroscope on the weapon. It was felt that fluoroscopy would give them sharper detail about the internal structure and function of the bomb, perhaps providing greater clues to its manufacture and origin. This proved fruitless and provided no help.

The x-ray from the fluoroscope did, however, trigger a small "toy" and initiate a silent countdown within the bomb, the first of Dr. Reisen's fail-safe devices implanted to assure detonation.

ISIS leader and commander, Abu Bakr, called the team tasked with disarming this weapon by cell phone periodically for updates. He was becoming more and more agitated with their failure to find a solution to disarming the bomb. A decision was made to attempt to physically turn the weapon ever so slightly to see if the writing on the hidden side could be identified. Realizing the danger inherent in moving any explosive device, the team spent a good deal of time in slowly clearing away parts of the rubble that surrounded it and then turning it with great care.

When that was accomplished, the writing on the bomb was clearly apparent. It was determined to be Yiddish, which shocked all of them. Finding someone in the ISIS compound who would admit to being able to translate Yiddish took some time.

"The words are 'the Sword of Ehud,'" the translator said.

"And who is this Ehud, another Jewish pig?" This from the chief technician.

"You must forgive me for having this knowledge," the translator said. "It comes from my previous Christian upbringing, which I have renounced."

"We understand that. You have nothing to fear. What does this Sword of Ehud mean?"

"Again, I apologize for even knowing this meaning. It comes from what Christians refer to as the Old Testament of their Bible, which the Jews, forgive me, call their Torah. It is from the Book of Judges. The man Ehud was a judge."

"Judges? What judges? What meaning does this have for us? And why would this weapon be named for a judge?"

"That I do not know, chief technician. In the story, which I am certain is filled with Jewish lies, the Jews have been attacked by their enemy, and Ehud is chosen to go to the enemy king with a gift. When he is alone with the king, he draws his sword, which has been hidden under his cloak, and slays him. Thus, the Sword of Ehud."

This story was immediately relayed to Bakr.

"Jews? This is a Jewish bomb? The Jews do not have a bomb of this size. Nor do they have an aircraft large enough to deliver it. Perhaps it was developed and dropped by the Americans. But we have clear intelligence that Israel has not been permitted to enter or assist in the war over concern of further angering the Arab nations. I fear no Jewish weapon. Disarm it at once. Our virus and atomic teams are inside Israel, exploding their weapons and destroying Jews even as we speak. Disarm this failed weapon of the pigs, or you will all face the consequences."

The technicians followed their previous knowledge of disarming bombs and began by trying to unscrew the nose cone. Turning the cone to the left, as was normally done to unscrew any similar device, was very difficult. The team was able to move the cone left only a small amount, which appeared to further tighten it. Turning it to the right did loosen the cone, and it was gently removed.

"The Jews are used to doing things backward," the chief technician said.

His team smiled nervously.

"Let us look at the wiring."

The wiring, too, was unlike any color sequence they had previously encountered. They had many Western armament technology volumes, which explained wiring systems and color coding, but none of them was helpful. Unfortunately, they did not have any similar Israeli manuals.

Suddenly their Geiger counters began to sound. Loudly.

The technicians backed away from the bomb and hurriedly called Bakr.

"Radioactive, you say? Are you telling me this is an atomic weapon?"

"Yes, my Caliph. What are your instructions?"

"My instructions are the same as before. Disarm the weapon, or you will regret your failure. It could be just a Jewish trick."

The technicians were baffled. They called for lead shielding while they tried to decipher the odd, color-coded wiring. But their time had run out. Their attempt to unscrew the nose cone by turning it to the left, the traditional way, had set off a timer, which would detonate the weapon in exactly eleven minutes. The number eleven equaled the total number of letters in the phrase *Sword of Ehud,* a bit of whimsy from

Dr. Reisen and the second of his fail-safe "toys." The first, triggered by the x-rays from the fluoroscope, took longer and would not be needed. Now, time was up and the "child" was ready to play.

The fifty-megaton explosion immediately vaporized the entire fourth level of the headquarters, including all personnel, viruses, atomic materials, and laboratories. The blast expanded in all directions and also incinerated the hospital on the third level, destroying all patients, medical personnel, and equipment.

On the second level, several classes in the Holy Quran and Sharia law were being taught, as well as two martial arts instruction sessions. The actors in a film about how teenagers in America could join ISIS were being recorded. They, too, were incinerated.

The powerful bomb's blast and radiation finally reached the first level, containing Abu Bakr's personal quarters, his bomb shelter, and the village with its inhabitants. Over one hundred slaves, who had recently been captured and were awaiting a lifetime of abject servitude and sexual molestation, were also disintegrated. They would never know what a true blessing this was.

Bakr and Ali were in the shelter enjoying two British teenage women who had recently fled their upper-class homes to join ISIS. They were all instantly transformed into less than dust. Ali's gold sword became nothing more than a radioactive golden nugget. All of these things happened in a matter of seconds.

The incredible strength of the bomb had not yet diminished. The child continued to want to play. The blast erupted from the earth into the atmosphere, propelling the traditional mushroom cloud several thousand feet into the sky. The desert sand was turned to glass for a half mile in all directions by the intense heat. Once again the three thousand year-old city of Dabiq, Muhammad's favorite, became a desert wasteland—a radioactive desert wasteland where no life would exist for another thousand years.

In all, the Sword of Ehud had immolated the hidden headquarters of ISIS, killing over three thousand human beings and destroying more than $50 million in highly specialized technical equipment of all types. The child had finished playing and was content. For the time being.

60

G ENERAL CHUCK CLARK WAS ON the phone in his temporary residence at a secure location close to the Pentagon. The small home he was in had recently been electronically swept and found to be free of any virus remnants and had not been close to any of the nuclear detonations.

"A nuclear explosion? You're sure? How large? Jesus. Fifty megs. You're sure? Must have been the Russians. No one else I know about has a bomb that big. And it was in the Syrian desert, you say? What was the target? What do you mean there was nothing there? The Ruskies wouldn't drop a bomb that size on nothing. Must be a hell of a lot of radiation. Fly a couple of drones over it and send me the latest photos. What else is going on? Nothing? How many times are you going to say nothing? No movements by anyone? No more attacks? Okay, inform the other Joint Chiefs and keep me updated." He hung up.

Now what the fuck was that all about and where was it headed?

What had been uppermost on Clark's mind was trying to figure out when he should move into the White House. Naturally, he wouldn't take over the Oval Office—at least not for a while. He didn't want to alarm the nation any more than it was already.

He had dismissed his aides for the time being and was ruminating over what to do about Dixie Colfax, the interim Joint Chiefs chairman who he had relieved. Colfax was in a protected room in the Pentagon, under twenty-four-hour guard. Clark felt that Dixie would come around, sooner or later, to the thinking of the other Joint Chiefs and would be given a responsible position in the new administration—Clark's administration. If he still wouldn't go along, well, Guantanamo was still open. It would be easy to simply make his old friend Dixie disappear.

The chiefs were working on an announcement for the general public about the present situation, emphasizing the temporary nature of the "management" of the government by the military until the presidential succession could be determined. Clark knew there would be no changes in the foreseeable future. And he thought the whole presidential succession thing was a joke.

The knock on the door startled him. He had purposely chosen this location so he'd have time to figure out his future plans, and only a few trusted men knew where he was. He checked the peephole and then opened the door to see a stunning woman he recognized immediately as former House Speaker Lucy Jennings.

"Mind if I come in, General?"

"Not at all, Madam Speaker," he said, opening the door further and allowing her to pass by him, perhaps a little closer than she needed to be.

Like everyone else in Washington, Clark knew Jennings' sexual reputation. He had testified before her about military matters on several occasions when she was in the House and had seen her at cocktail parties and restaurants as well—always with a different man. He had heard rumors that she was seeing Chief Justice Arnie Mason and wondered what she was doing here now.

"Please sit down, Madam Speaker." Clark gestured to a chair. "These are not my usual quarters, and I don't know what's comfortable yet."

Lucy walked slowly across the room and sat down. "This will be fine, General. And please call me Lucy. I promise not to take up too much of your time." Actually, Jennings had decided to spend the rest of the day with Clark, and the night too. It was all part of her strategy.

Clark sat across from her and took in the total picture. She was really very attractive. "Oh, by the way, how did you find my location, Lucy? I've been keeping pretty quiet about these temporary digs."

Lucy chuckled. "When you've been in Washington as long as I have, General, you develop sources."

"I see. Now how can I help you?"

Lucy took a deep breath, which she knew would get Clark's attention where she wanted it. "General—may I call you Chuck? Chuck, I understand you and the other Joint Chiefs have taken over ... let's call it 'administration' of the government."

Clark hesitated with his reply. No formal public announcement had been made, and he wondered, again, how this woman knew so much about highly sensitive, confidential issues. "And who told you that, Madam ... uh, Lucy?"

"The same sources, Chuck. I'd just like to say that it's about time someone who understands government and power was running the country. In my opinion, this should have been done two years ago when that woman was appointed acting president."

Clark nodded. "It's good to know how you feel, Lucy. I happen to agree with your thoughts about Rose Akron. It's a shame though that President Dansby had so little time in office and experienced such a tragic death." This was a test to see how committed Jennings really was to the Joint Chiefs takeover. She wanted something, and this might bring her out.

"I'd have to disagree about Dansby, Chuck. I heard he wasn't even a natural born citizen. And, frankly, I didn't think he was that powerful or effective during his time in the Senate. By the way, would it be possible for me to have a drink?"

"Certainly, Lucy," Clark said, standing up and walking over to a bar. "I don't know how well stocked this place is, but let's take a look. What's your pleasure?"

"Scotch, please. Neat. And I hope you'll join me."

"I'd be glad to do that," Clark said, realizing this was much more than a simple meeting. He walked back over to her and handed her the drink.

She stood up and clinked glasses with him. "To better government," she said and drained her glass. She moved up close to him. Very close. Close enough to kiss. And he did. Then again.

"Is there any more scotch?" she said, continuing to press up against him. She could feel his body reacting as she expected.

"I think I can find some," he said, reluctant to move away from her.

When their glasses were filled again, they stood looking at each other. "Chuck, isn't there a more comfortable place we can get to know each other better?"

He took her hand, and they walked into the bedroom. Once again, Lucy felt at home. She was in charge.

Two hours later, they were both relaxing in bed. Lucy was mentally going over what she was going to say to Clark about her plan. The general was yet another man who had met his match and was completely captivated by Lucy Jennings. He'd had women from all over the world during his career but never anyone like Lucy.

"Chuck, I want to talk to you seriously about the future—yours and mine."

"This is a great time for it, Lucy. Frankly, I couldn't move if I wanted to. And I don't want to."

"Good, Chuck. Neither do I." She stared at him, and he suddenly had the distinct feeling he was in great danger.

"I know there are things about the present governmental situation that you don't want to—and can't—discuss. I understand all that, and I won't press you on it. I also know you've been in the military most of your adult life and spent a good deal of time in Washington. But you don't know politics in this town, Chuck—not the way I do. I know every secret held by every high government official, and I can get anything I want done in Washington, quickly and efficiently."

"I've heard about your ... uh ... effectiveness, Lucy."

"I'm sure you have. All of those stories are true. I get what I want. It may take some time, but I get it. The point is that you're going to have to do some fancy maneuvering in the near future to maintain your position and power and stay in charge. I can do more than help. I can make it happen."

Clark considered this. He knew that Jennings was telling the truth about her Washington know-how. He also knew that he would be facing some stiff challenges and serious criticism about his "military takeover." Lucy could be valuable—in many ways. "Lucy, I hear what you're saying, and I'm interested. It would help me if I knew what you were after."

Lucy gave him a glance that made him shiver—him, a twenty-eight-year air force veteran who had been shot down over Afghanistan and survived being tortured for eight months in a Taliban prison. This was no ordinary woman.

"What I want is simple, Chuck. I want to be president of the United States, and I don't care what I have to do to get there. Now, listen to me. Sooner or later, you're going to have to make a change in your present … um … status. This country, its people, its politics, and the Supreme Court will never stand for a—and forgive me for this, Chuck—they'll never stand for a military junta taking over a government created by Washington and Jefferson and preserved by Lincoln. You need to have a backup plan. I'm your backup."

"And you're going to explain to me exactly how all this is going to work," he said, rolling closer to her.

After the two of them had showered and were back in the living room, glasses of scotch in hand, Lucy began. "So here's a logical outline for the future, Chuck. We'll both know the right time for this to happen. While the war continues and the country is in crisis, I'm guessing that the people will feel safer and more secure with the Joint Chiefs in power. There will be complaints, and you can bet the liberals will raise holy hell about you not following the presidential succession. My suggestion is that, when the hue and cry dies down, a prime time will present itself for you and the chiefs to come forward and announce that you are establishing a transition back to civilian leadership and an eventual presidential election, by appointing, let's say, an acting president.

"Because Rose Akron was acting president, the people will recognize and feel comfortable with that title. Depending on the status of Congress—we don't know now how many House and Senate members have been killed or injured by the ISIS attacks—depending on that, it may even be possible to have Congress appoint the acting president again. After all, that title is in the Constitution."

Clark followed all of Lucy's scenario with great interest. What a mind this woman had!

"And this acting president would be?" he asked.

"That would be me, Chuck, as I'm sure you guessed."

"I did, but I wanted to hear you say it." Chuck swallowed more scotch.

Another woman president? That was at the root of all of the country's problems as far as he was concerned. How would Lucy Jennings be any better? Still, her proposal had some merit in several ways.

Almost reading his mind, Lucy began again. "There are many advantages to this game plan, Chuck. It takes the Joint Chiefs out of the spotlight. You're still there, and you're still the power behind the throne, so to speak. But now the country would have a visible figurehead with the word *president* in her title. While it wouldn't take a constitutional genius to point out the continuing … uh … unauthorized procedures in my appointment, it appears to be a move toward constitutionality. That's especially true if we can get Congress to make the appointment. Leave that to me."

"What about the Supreme Court, Lucy? I hear you may have some expertise in that area."

Jennings nodded. "You could call it that, Chuck. Yes, I think I can promise you that this move would receive tacit approval by the court, with the understanding that this was only a first step toward full constitutionality. And, as a further protection for you and the other chiefs, I can promise a quick presidential pardon should anyone try to bring charges against you at any point."

"Sounds like you have it all figured out, Lucy. And pretty well put together, I must say. One other thing bothers me. What about presidential succession? There are bound to be cabinet members still out there."

"That's another thing I like about a military man being in charge, Chuck. Get rid of them."

"I beg your pardon?"

"Make them disappear, Chuck. Need I be more specific?"

Clark was sure his shiver was noticeable this time. "No, I guess not."

"There's one more thing, Chuck. And it's not inconsequential."

"What's that?"

"Me. You'd have me. Exclusively. And while no one can keep secrets for long in this town, I can promise you that our relationship would be discreet and confidential as much as possible. We wouldn't live together; in fact, we'd seldom be seen together outside of government functions. I think you know I'm not the clingy type. I have plenty of money, and I get along well on my own."

Chuck nodded. "And what happens after this interim period where you would be acting president?"

"Then I'm on my own. There will be a regular presidential election eventually to get us back on course, and I take my own chances when that happens. You are either still head of the Joint Chiefs, or you could choose to retire, protected by my pardon powers."

***

It would be interesting to look inside the minds of both of these people. Chuck Clark was certain he would never give up power to anyone. A military government was just what the American people needed at this time, and he would give it to them. He'd hang on to Lucy, too, for as long as he wanted. Women were a dime a dozen. This one was clever and would take careful handling. And he could always do to her what she wanted him to do to the cabinet members. Accidents happened all the time. So did assassinations.

Lucy Jennings dreamed of having all the power she ever wanted once she was appointed president. She'd use that power as she saw fit, with a weakened Congress unable to stop her—if there even was a Congress. Sure, she'd think about pardoning the Joint Chiefs for their illegal and immoral act of taking over the government. Maybe. It would depend on how quickly Clark and his cronies turned things over to her. And whether or not she felt like it. Yes, this was her time—time for President Lucy Jennings.

Printed in the United States
By Bookmasters